PUCKING HARDENED HEARTS

PUCKING DARK HEARTS
BOOK 3

MAGGIE ALABASTER

Copyright © 2024 by Maggie Alabaster

All rights reserved.

No part of this book may be reproduced in any form or by any electronic or mechanical means, including information storage and retrieval systems, without written permission from the author, except for the use of brief quotations in a book review.

Cover design by Artscandare

Edited by Lily Luchesi

Proofread by Nora Hogan

CHAPTER 1
EDEN

I came with a roll of my hips and a raw, low moan.

My back arched. I clawed at the blankets with my long, manicured nails. My head tipped back and I saw stars.

So many stars in my otherwise blackened vision. My body was lost in pure bliss. A perfect moment that lasted forever, and never long enough.

Slowly, I drifted back down to Earth.

Gradually, I loosened my grip on the blankets, rocked my hips in an easy rhythm, encouraging, pushing, until Mitch came. Pounding once, twice, before spilling himself inside my body.

In turn, Mitch stole an orgasm from Jagger.

The other centre knelt behind him, sliding smoothly in and out of his rear hole. He groaned and grunted, grinding out every drop of pleasure and release.

Mitch sagged forward, breathing heavily until he regained his breath.

"Fucking hell," he breathed. "That was awesome." He looked down at me and grinned, blue eyes shining like they always did. The only time he didn't smile was when he was on the rink. Then, his eyes were twin chips of ice in a mask of concentration. If the world ended while he held a hockey stick in his hand, he'd never notice.

"It wasn't bad," Jagger said. He slid out of Mitch and flopped down beside me. The bed dipped and shivered under his weight. At six-foot-five, he didn't do anything small. "Thanks."

He rolled off the bed and started to gather up his clothes.

"Hey, it was better than not bad." Mitch squinted at him.

"Yeah, it was good." Jagger shrugged.

Mitch slid his cock out of me and joined Jagger in the search for his clothes. "Don't give too many compliments, will you?" His tone was slightly sarcastic, but unruffled. He was used to Jagger's permanent underwhelm.

Jagger chuckled. "Never." He scooped up Mitch's T-shirt and flicked it at him. "Don't want you getting a big head."

Mitch caught the shirt and pulled it over his head.

"He wouldn't say anything bad about us." I sat up

and pulled my knees together. "He enjoys fucking us too much."

I spoke lightly too, trying to keep the bitterness from my tone, but the way they both hopped up so quickly to leave… They did the same thing every time. It shouldn't sting, but it did. The reaction was stupid. Irrational. We weren't in a relationship. This was sex, nothing more. I knew that. So did they. The arrangement suited us.

And yet, if they wanted to stick around for longer, I'd be okay with that. I didn't expect them to stay around all night, but they didn't have to rush out so quickly either. Did they?

Mitch grinned. "Accurate. That's because we're both so irresistible."

I resisted the urge to say Jagger only liked us because we put out. Instead, I pulled the blankets over myself. I needed a shower. That would wait until after they left. What time they'd give me, I'd savour.

"Yes, you are." Jagger grabbed the front of Mitch's T-shirt and yanked him forward to kiss his mouth. He pulled back and leaned over to do the same to me. "We have morning skate tomorrow. We better go."

Jagger was the centre for the Opal Springs Ghouls ice hockey team, and Mitch was his alternate. We often joked about me being in the middle of a centre sandwich, but they were as hands on with each other as they were with me. Their relationship with each other was as casual as the one with me. They worked together and they fucked. They were friends, but that was all.

For now.

"You good?" Mitch waited until Jagger stepped aside to pull on his track pants, before he leaned over to kiss me.

I knew better than to think he was concerned. He always asked me the same question. It was a habit at this point.

I always responded the same way. "Yep, I'm good."

Sometimes, I wanted to broach the subject of our relationship, or lack thereof, but I didn't want to ruin what we had. We all made it clear from the start that we were nothing more than fuck buddies. For almost two years, we'd been just that. Exclusive fuck buddies. End of story.

I asked myself what changed for me, but I couldn't put my finger on it. Maybe it was seeing my two best friends, Cat and Marley, settling down with their boyfriends and having children. I had no intention of having kids, but they had three boyfriends each. Men who thought they hung the moon. Men who didn't fuck and run.

A girl couldn't help feeling a *little* envious.

"Are you sure?" Mitch pressed gently. "You look... I don't know."

"I'm tired," I said quickly. "I could use a holiday." The last one I had, Marley and I went to the Gold Coast to give her a break from the man trouble she was having at the time. She and her guys worked everything out, but for a while there, things were tense.

"You should take one," Jagger said. "Everyone needs a break once in a while. Go away somewhere warm and enjoy yourself."

Of course, he didn't suggest either of them would go with me. Even if we had that kind of relationship, they were right at the start of hockey season. They wouldn't have a real break for months. Most of their attention would be focused on training, travelling and playing. With the occasional fuck squeezed in here or there.

"Things are busy at work," I said.

They weren't really. Winter was always slow for my florist shop. Most of my time was occupied with taking bookings for spring and summer weddings, and placing orders for next year's Valentine's Day.

Jagger shrugged. "Okay, well. Some other time." He sat on the end of the bed and pulled on his sneakers. "I'll see you later." To Mitch he said, "Coming?"

"Yeah." Mitch gave me another look and a smile before pushing his feet into his own shoes and stepping away from the bed. "Thanks, it was fun, like always." He gave me another quick kiss before they both slipped from my bedroom and out the front door.

"Yeah, fun," I said to the empty room.

Outside, the engine of Jagger's car roared to life and headed off down the road.

With an impatient shove, I pushed the covers off and headed into the shower to rinse off the sweat from my body, and the cum that trickled down the insides of my thighs. I washed my short, purple hair, stepped out of the shower and grabbed a towel to dry off.

I draped my towel over the rail on the wall and pulled on a pair of bright pink track pants and the black T-shirt I slept in. Perched where Jagger sat not ten minutes earlier, I pulled on fluffy purple bed socks and slipped out to the kitchen.

I flipped on the electric kettle that sat on the white quartz countertop, and readied a mug for hot chocolate.

"Your friends are gone?" Brock Edwards stepped through the door that led to the garage, and tossed his keys on the kitchen island. Employed as a security guard for various locations, including the Ghouls' arena, he worked irregular hours.

"You just missed them." I grabbed another mug out of the cupboard after he nodded to my silent question, and added hot chocolate powder to his.

Technically, he owned the house, having bought out my mother after their divorce. He let me live here too, even though he wasn't my stepfather anymore. The place was big enough that we didn't get in each other's way, and it was close to my work.

I worried my mother would think I was taking sides, but she hadn't said anything. Not to me anyway. She moved on so quickly, she probably didn't give the situation a second thought. Now living in Sydney, she was already engaged to some property developer. She seemed happy. Settled. More so than when she lived here.

I didn't know why she'd left, and Brock never brought it up. He closed the door on that chapter in his life and put it behind him. I'd decided a long time ago not to ask. If he wanted to share, he would.

"Shame." Brock leaned against the island and watched me make hot chocolate.

"Why's that?" I glanced over to see his gaze lingering in the region of my breasts. My face heated and I turned back to finish stirring our drinks.

"They seem nice." He reached over to pick up his drink, his hand brushing my arm before he gripped the mug and stepped back.

"Yeah, nice." I wrapped my fingers around my mug and inhaled the chocolatey scent before I took a sip.

"Have you had enough of nice?" He gave the impression he was asking for a particular reason.

I decided it was better not to suggest he elaborate on that either.

"No, I just…" I turned to lean my back against the countertop.

"You want more?" He sipped his own drink and nodded his approval at the taste. "Let me guess, they don't want that."

I sighed out my nose. "I don't know what I want. We all agreed we didn't want a commitment. But sometimes I'd like to—I don't know—have an *actual* relationship."

"Have you told them that?" he asked, eyebrows elevated slightly. "Or is it that you don't want an actual relationship with *them?* Or you can't choose which one you want a relationship with? From what I can tell, they seem tight." He wasn't passing judgment, just stating a fact.

"They are," I agreed. "They're best friends. Best friends with benefits."

"So, they're a package deal?" Brock asked. "Are you worried if you try to choose one, they'll end up choosing each other?"

"All of the above." I ran a hand over the back of my head, tangling my fingers in my hair. "I don't know, maybe I should end things with them. Give them a chance to find someone they want to be with."

"Is that what you want?" Brock looked at me more intently.

"Not really," I admitted. "Am I being a brat? I have things really good with them, but it's not enough. Maybe I'm being fussy. I mean, how many girls have two hot hockey players who want to…" I cleared my throat.

Brock was only my stepfather for a handful of years, but talking about sex with him was awkward for me. I mean, him and my mother would have…

Yeah, better not finish that thought. I didn't have any brain bleach.

Brock, on the other hand, didn't hold back. "Fuck you? I can think of two more women, off the top of my head, who have partners on the same team: Cat and Marley."

Of course, he'd known my friends almost as long as I had. "If Mitch and Jagger can't give you what you need, they might have friends who can."

"That wouldn't be awkward at all," I said sarcastically. "Asking them to introduce me to someone else." I took another sip of my rapidly cooling drink.

"Awkward for them, or for you?" he asked. "If you want to be with them, you should tell them that. If they decide to walk, that's their loss." After a moment he added, "Do you think they'd walk away?"

I considered the question. Shook my head and shrugged. "I don't know. They might want to leave things the way they are."

"You don't have to do that if you don't want to," he reminded me. "You're allowed to decide for yourself if that isn't what you want." He paused for a moment. "Let me ask you this. How would you feel if they wanted to be with you? Is that the real issue here? You're scared they might agree to a relationship outside the bedroom?"

"I…" I hadn't considered that. The scenarios that crossed my mind were either: I wouldn't say anything, or if I did, they'd walk away. Not for a moment had I considered they might be in for anything more. Not really.

When Brock cocked his head at me, I realised I hadn't given him an answer.

"I guess so," I conceded. "Everything would change.

For one thing, they'd be here more often. Or I'd be at their place more often."

They shared a small house near the ice hockey arena. Separate bedrooms. As far as I knew, they didn't touch each other unless they were with me. Outside of my bedroom, they were friends and workmates. Buddies.

For some reason, Brock looked irritated at that idea. "They're welcome here." He set down his mug and stepped closer. "I don't mind listening to you."

His words hung between us for the longest time, becoming thick enough to touch, as they gradually worked their way into my brain.

Listening to me? Holy shit.

My face was so hot it must have been flaming red. I swallowed down my mouthful of hot chocolate before I choked.

"Wouldn't that be awkward?" I muttered.

He brushed hair off the side of my face with his knuckle and leaned in closer. "Not at all," he whispered. "I want to hear you getting off. Next time they want to come over, make sure I'm here. I want to hear you cry out."

"Brock," I said softly. My whole body was trembling in response to the nearness of his. "We shouldn't…"

His lips brushed over my cheek. He whispered, "I'm not married to your mother anymore."

He stepped away and grabbed both our mugs to put

them in the dishwasher before he headed into his own room.

I leaned against the counter for a little while, looking at his closed door before I headed to bed.

CHAPTER 2
EDEN

"Hey." I slipped into the chair beside Cat and Marley.

Once a month, we got together for lunch. Their boyfriends would look after their children so we could have some girl time. The days when we met up at O'Reilly's pub for a few drinks, then a few more, were behind us. Behind them, anyway.

Now, they were both mothers. Getting drunk on the weekend wasn't a priority anymore. Spending time with their families was.

That wasn't the reason I never wanted children. Okay, that wasn't the *only* reason. Their kids were cute, but I had zero maternal instincts. No biological clock ticking away, ready to explode. I was happy being kid-free.

"Hey." Marley leaned over to give me a hug. "You look tired."

I grimaced. "Shouldn't that be my line?"

"Lucky for me, Declan sleeps through the night. He has since he was six months old." She shook her napkin out onto her lap and picked up a menu.

"So does Sophie," Cat said. "Although, now we're entering the terrible twos, things are…interesting." She grimaced, but in that she-didn't-really-mind-a-bit way.

"I've heard about those," Marley said.

I picked up a menu and scanned it while they talked about their children. Since I had nothing meaningful to add, I said nothing. I listened and quietly added to my long list of reasons I'd never join them in motherhood.

"I'm sorry, listen to us go on and on." Marley shot me an apologetic look. "We didn't mean to bore you."

"You didn't bore me," I said quickly. "I don't mind hearing about them, really."

I was Aunt Eden, by friendship if not by blood. Of course I cared about the little ones, but my friends had motherhood in common. A bond I'd never share with them. Sometimes I felt like the third wheel on a brightly coloured bicycle. One that would never become a tricycle.

"I want to know how things are going with you." Cat reached over and patted my hand. A stunning redhead, she used to be a speed skater. Now she was a full-time veterinarian, looking after the spoiled pets of Opal Springs.

"Things are fine," I said. "You know what they say, same shit, different day. Work is work."

"Cat wants to know about your love life," Marley

said. She laughed when Cat gave her a sideways look. "Okay, so do I. Have Jagger and Mitch admitted they're head over balls for you yet?"

She swatted at me when I gave her a funny look. "You know it's true. We've seen the way they look at you. Haven't we, Cat?"

"Yes, we have," Cat agreed. "Easton was saying the other day that it was obvious to everyone but them."

"Apparently I didn't see it either," I said dryly. Trying not to look too hopeful, I added, "You really think they feel that way about me?"

"They'd be stupid if they didn't," Marley said firmly. "But how do *you* feel?"

I told them about the conversation I'd had with Brock a couple of nights earlier. Not the last bit, of course. In a handful of words, I reiterated what he said about Mitch and Jagger.

As for the rest, I was still trying to get my head around Brock suggesting he wanted to listen to me being fucked. I couldn't decide if I was aroused, disturbed, or somewhere in between. He was right, he wasn't my stepfather anymore, but he *used* to be. Surely there were rules against things like that?

On the other hand, my mother had moved on, why shouldn't he? Should that be with me though? The thoughts that thundered through my head threatened to make me dizzy.

"If it was me, I'd go for it," Marley said, breaking

through my wild thoughts. "Life is too short not to grab it by the balls and get the most out of it."

"Marley is right," Cat said. "If they're into you and you're into them, what do you have to lose?"

"Everything if you're wrong," I said with a sigh. "I could tell them I want a relationship with them, and they could shut me down. Considering how busy they are with training and games and—everything. Who's to say they have time for me?"

"If they care about you, they'll *make* time," Cat said firmly. "Remember when I met Shaw, Cruz and Easton? They were all working full-time jobs, balancing those with training and playing, and working towards the team going professional. They still had time for me."

"I remember," I said. Cruz and Easton weren't nice to her in the beginning, but they'd come around. Of course they had, she was awesome. Anyone could see that.

"I'm with Cat, if they want you, they'll make time," Marley said firmly.

"It still seems like a pretty big 'if' to me," I said doubtfully.

The server stopped beside the table to take our orders before hurrying away to the kitchen.

"I could ask them for you," Marley offered. "Or one of the guys could."

Two of her boyfriends were on the same team as Jagger and Mitch. Toby was the Ghouls' goalie, while Cole was a defenceman. Her third boyfriend, Oliver, was a doctor, and Cat's father.

In the past, there was friction over Marley being with him, but she and Cat put it behind them and moved on. Fortunately for all concerned. For a while there, things looked like they might get ugly.

"Hell no," I said quickly. "That would be all sorts of awkward. Not to mention, we put high school behind us a long time ago. No more passing notes with checkboxes for guys to tick 'yes' or 'no' if they wanted to go out with us or not."

Marley pointed a pink-nailed finger at me. "That method was effective. I got at least four or five boyfriends that way."

"How long did they last?" Cat asked, a smile tugging at the corners of her lips.

"The average was three or four days," Marley said, eyes shining. "The longest lasted for a week and a half. That was practically married at that age." She laughed.

We both joined her.

I fondly remembered those days. Now, we were too mature to pass around notes, and giggle over boys, but some things hadn't changed. I still had no idea if they wanted to go out with me or not.

Now I thought about it, maybe Marley had a point. Giving Jagger and Mitch a note like that would give them a good laugh. On the other hand, that laugh would be at my expense, so I dismissed the idea.

"I thought things were supposed to be simpler when we got older," I said with a sigh. "Meet some incredible guy, fall in love and all that shit. It seems to me like everything gets more and more complicated." Especially with Brock adding a twist to our relationship.

"We spend our entire childhoods wanting to grow up and our entire adulthoods wanting to be children again," Marley said wistfully. "Sometimes I envy Declan. He has at least four or five years to enjoy himself before he has to worry about school and responsibility. Right now, all he cares about is eating, drinking, sleeping and listening to his fathers read him stories. That's the life."

"All Sophie cares about is eating chicken nuggets for breakfast, lunch and dinner," Cat said. "The only time she'll eat anything else is when Shaw gives it to her."

Her expression softened as she spoke. She clearly adored her two-year-old daughter and her boyfriends. Of course she did, they were all good for each other. A perfect little family unit. Sophie and Declan were both growing up surrounded by so much love.

Not to mention, so many opportunities to find a parent who would say 'yes' when all the others said 'no.' It wouldn't be long before they figured that one out.

"I can relate to that," I said. "Sometimes I want to eat chicken nuggets for every meal too. Or chocolate. Actually, the best thing about being an adult is that I can do that."

If I wanted to eat cake for breakfast, I could do that too. And yet, I was scared of having a conversation with two grown men I was intimate with. To be fair though, cake was a lot easier than men. Cake didn't judge you or turn you down. It just sat there and let you eat it. That made it pretty reasonable, if you asked me. No wonder everyone loved cake so much. It basically loved us too.

"If I did that, Sophie would want chocolate all day, every day." Cat grimaced.

"She's stubborn like her mother," Marley teased.

"She's stubborn like her *grandfather*," Cat retorted.

Marley made a face at her. Evidently she hadn't entirely come to terms with the fact one of her boyfriends was a grandfather. Oliver, on the other hand, loved being both a grandfather and a father of a young son. He took all of it in stride.

While they teased each other, my mind wandered to Brock. He was only a couple of years younger than Oliver. Also old enough to be a grandfather. He had a son a couple of years younger than me whom he rarely saw. No grandchildren. Yet. None that I knew of anyway.

Should that put me off considering his request? Possibly, but the idea of my former stepfather listening to me fucking was arousing as hell. Was that fucked up?

I decided I didn't care. We were all consenting adults. If he was still married to my mother, it would be weird and wrong, but as he pointed out, he wasn't. The only obstacle was that Mitch and Jagger might not want to be overheard.

That was a conversation for later.

"So are you going to?" Marley asked.

I turned to her and blinked. I got the impression she'd been waiting a minute or two for an answer. I must have completely switched off. If the throbbing in my pussy and the dampness in my panties was any indication, I'd phased out for a while.

"Sorry," I said. "Am I going to what?"

"Skate naked in the middle of the arena," Marley said, completely deadpan.

I blinked again. "Why would I—" When she started to smile, I realised she hadn't asked me anything like that. She'd noticed my mind was off somewhere else.

I swatted her arm. "What did you really ask?"

"Marley wanted to know if you're going to talk to Mitch and Jagger," Cat supplied. "About having a relationship." She spoke in a patient tone, equally appropriate for addressing her daughter or her animal patients.

"Oh." I should have guessed that was what she asked. "I might. When the time is right. Who's skating naked?" I didn't think anyone was, but it was a good way to deflect the conversation away from me. Not to mention the visual image was pleasant. Men skating around the rink, their cocks dangling between their thighs. All of that toned muscle, firm asses on display.

They should take photos and make a calendar. I'd buy a copy or two. One for home and one for work.

"That sounds like something Cruz, Easton and Toby would all do, given half a chance," Marley said. "Probably Oliver too." He was a speed skater in the past, like Cat. He could give the other guys a run for their money, if he wanted to.

Cat made a face and stuck out her tongue. "Ewww. The last thing I want to see is my father naked." She shook her head like she might shake the thought away completely.

"Thank fuck for that," Marley said. "That would be weird. Right, Eden?"

"Right," I agreed. "No one wants to see their own father naked." If they did, that was their business, but I certainly didn't. I hadn't seen mine at all since I was about ten, when he checked out on me and Mum. As for seeing Brock naked…

I swallowed.

I shouldn't think things like that. He was my mother's ex. Didn't that make him out of bounds? Should I have turned his request down flat?

I scratched my ear like I did whenever I was anxious. It was my nervous tic, and right now I was on edge as hell. Thinking about Brock made my pulse ratchet up like crazy. If I was honest, he'd had that effect on me for a long time. I never thought I'd acknowledge it, much less act on it.

Fuck, what the hell was I getting myself into?

CHAPTER 3
EDEN

"Hey, gorgeous."

At the sound of the familiar voice, I straightened up from my warmup stretches and turned to look behind me.

Jagger and Mitch stood side by side on the footpath, dressed in light track pants and Ghouls' hoodies. Both looked good enough to eat. Okay, when did they not?

"Hey." I managed to sound cool, normal. My heart pounded like crazy. "Fancy meeting you guys here."

It wasn't as though I didn't know where they did their morning runs and when. I'd joined them often enough. Casual and easy, friends out for exercise. Should I keep it that way? Did I really want to risk fucking them up?

"Yeah, what a coincidence," Jagger said dryly.

Like always, Mitch smiled and leaned over to fix his shoelace. "You coming running with us?"

"I thought I might," I said lightly. How could they not see through me right now? I was almost certain I was displaying all of my inner thoughts and turmoil right there on my face.

And yet, they didn't seem to notice.

Mitch glanced up and grinned. "Great. It's always more fun when it's the three of us. Right, Jag?"

"Yep, sure," Jagger said with his usual noncommittal tone and half shrug. Arm's length and no closer, at least emotionally.

"I don't have to run with you if you don't want me to," I said tentatively.

"I said it was fine, didn't I?" Jagger said sharply. "If I didn't want you along, I would have said so." He looked from Mitch to me and back again. "Are we running or what?"

Mitch rose. "We are running. Let's do this." He gave me a wink and started off at a slow trot, leaving me and Jagger to catch up.

I glanced at Jagger before hurrying to run beside Mitch, not wanting to get left behind.

Jagger settled into a slower pace right behind us.

"It's a nice day for it," I remarked. In spite of the bite of cold in the air, the sun was shining and the sky was clear. A perfect autumn morning.

"Small talk?" Mitch teased. "Okay, out with it."

"What makes you think there's anything to come out with?" I replied.

Of course he noticed. He'd probably seen it on my

face the moment they saw me. He was warm and friendly, not oblivious.

"Because you don't engage in small talk unless there's something wrong," he said. "You're the one who said you think it's a waste of time. That we should have more deep and meaningful conversations."

"I don't think that's exactly what I said." I increased my pace as he did.

"Close enough." He slid a look over to me and raised an eyebrow. "Go on, what is it? You know we only bite when you want us to."

Yes, they did, and they did it very well. Of course, now the exercise wasn't the only cause of the increase in my heart rate. Both of them knew exactly how to get me going with the slightest glance, the right words. They didn't even need to touch me.

"It's…" This was my last chance to do this or not. I could chicken out and tell them something else. I could skip right to Brock's request.

I took as deep a breath as I could manage, given we were running. Passing out from lack of oxygen wasn't part of my plan.

"This friends with benefits thing is great," I started. "You guys are awesome."

"Fuck, yeah we are," Jagger said. "If that was all you wanted to say—"

I looked back over my shoulder at him before turning around to face forward again. It would be just my luck to faceplant on the footpath because I wasn't looking where I was going. That was also not a part of my plan.

"It's not," I said quickly. "I think I want more."

"You *think* you want more?" Mitch asked. He frowned, seemingly confused.

"I *know* I want more," I corrected. "I don't just want to be fuck buddies with you both. I'm ready for an actual relationship."

"With which one of us?" Jagger sounded annoyed. More than that, he sounded pissed off.

I slowed to a walk so I could look at them both. "I don't want to choose."

They both matched my pace, although I was the only one starting to breathe more heavily. A couple of minutes of slow jog was nothing to guys as fit as them.

"If you don't want to choose, then…" Mitch frowned, letting the implications sink into his mind.

"I want both of you," I said. "And I don't want you to choose between each other and me. I care about both of you and I think you care about each other."

"Jag is all right," Mitch said with a laugh.

Jagger snorted. "Mitch is a prick, but he has his moments."

I'd be worried if I thought they were serious, but they shared a glance that confirmed what I already knew. Their feelings also ran deeper than fuck buddies.

"So, how does this work?" Jagger asked. "Theoretically." He gave us both the side eye.

"Theoretically, we go out on dates," I said. "We hang out together and see how things go."

"And we fuck?" Mitch asked.

"And we fuck," I agreed.

"Huh," Jagger grunted. "What happens if *we* don't want more?"

His question sank in and my heart sank with it.

"I don't know," I admitted. "I don't know if I can keep going the way we are. My feelings for both of you go beyond friendship. If you don't feel the same way, then… Then it might be best for me to walk away."

I took a couple of literal steps away. I was *not* going to cry, not until I was out of sight. Eden Wright didn't cry in front of other people.

Mitch reached out with one of his long arms and grabbed hold of my wrist. "Eden, wait. What if we do want this?" He looked meaningfully at Jagger. "I mean, we all get along really well, don't we? We know we're sexually compatible."

His grip on my wrist was firm and comforting, but he was quick to let go and let his hand drop against his muscular thigh.

I got the impression he felt like he was walking a tightrope between me and Jagger, mindful he might fall. Apparently he didn't feel like there was a safety net underneath him. Instead, he was trying to keep his balance.

Jagger made a sound that could have been in agreement but I wasn't completely sure. He looked like he couldn't decide if he should step all the way onto the boat, or jump back onto shore and bolt.

I had considered the possibility one of the guys would be agreeable to trying this out while the other wasn't, but I had no idea how to move forward from it. I didn't want to come between them, but I didn't want my heart broken either.

"What are you thinking?" I asked Jagger.

He shook his head slowly. "Fucked if I know. I thought we were all happy with our arrangement. If it ain't broken, don't fix it, and all that shit." His jaw clenched as though he was ready to bite some rocks and chew them into dust.

"We were happy with it," Mitch said. "But if Eden needs more from us, I don't see why we can't try. Plenty of the guys on the team have relationships like this. Who's to say we can't do it too?" He spread his hands out to either side, like it was that simple.

Other people did it, so it must not be a big deal.

Except that it *was* a big deal, and we all knew it.

Jagger squinted at me. "Are you going to want another guy or two?"

Would I? I couldn't deny Brock had gotten under my skin somewhat with his request. But an actual relationship with him? That was something I hadn't considered until now. Should I be considering it at all? He hadn't suggested we might be any more than what we already were, only the added bonus of him being in the stands, listening and cheering us on.

I shrugged one shoulder. "I don't know. Can we try this out and then see what the future holds?"

It was Jagger's turn to shrug. "I don't know. You're going to have to give me some time to think about it. When I get my head around it, I'll let you know." He nodded with finality before sliding past me and Mitch and breaking into a run.

I watched his back for a few moments before resuming the slow jog.

Mitch trotted beside me. "I'm guessing that wasn't the response you were hoping for?"

"Not exactly," I agreed. "But I did spring it on you both. I can't expect you to know what you want immediately. Not when we've continued the way we have for so long. Things were comfortable, and easy."

"They were," he agreed. "But sooner or later, something was going to give. One of us was going to either want more, or want to walk away."

"Is that greedy of me?" I asked. "Plenty of women would have felt privileged to be in my position."

Mitch grinned at my use of the word 'position.' Of course he did. Sometimes I thought he was nothing more than an overgrown teenager. That was one of the things I liked about him. He didn't take life too seriously, and nothing got him down for long. He was the most easygoing guy I'd ever met.

"I don't think it's greedy to want love," he said. "Sex is great, and all, but it's not everything."

I raised my eyebrows at him. "Did I just hear you

say that? Mitch Ward, centre for the Opal Springs Ghouls, thinks there's more to life than sex? Next thing you'll tell me there are women out there who aren't puck bunnies."

He laughed. "If you tell anyone I said that, I'll deny it. Lucky for me, there's no one else around to hear."

"I heard," I said. "And I happen to agree with you. Sex is fantastic, but it's not everything." I wanted great sex and great love, like my friends seemed to have. Was that too much to ask?

"For the record, I care about you too." He was starting to get slightly breathless. "Jagger also does, just give him some time. He's not good with change. Once he realises this is a good idea, he'll be on board."

"Yeah," I said without conviction.

I wasn't as sure about that. Jagger might just as easily walk away. If he did, who would he walk away from? Just me, or Mitch as well? If that happened, it would be all my fault. I would have been the one who ruined everything for them and for myself.

I felt like the instigator of one of those Internet threads, where the person asks if they were the asshole or not. Chances were, the Internet would agree that I was, in fact, the asshole. Why else would I not be satisfied with what I had? Maybe I wasn't meant to be loved like that. My father walked away, then my mother, why shouldn't everyone else?

"Come on, let's catch up to him," Mitch said. He increased his speed, but not so fast that I couldn't keep up. He was thoughtful that way. Fierce and violent on the ice, but sweet and charming off it. He could have had his choice of puck bunnies, but somehow he'd found Jagger and me.

Or I thought he had.

I couldn't shake the feeling that I'd screwed up. Maybe Mitch was just being nice to me until this run was done. If Jagger wanted nothing to do with me, then Mitch might also make the same decision for himself. They could find themselves a new woman to be their fuck buddy. Or several of them. Why stick to just one, especially when anyone else might also start to develop feelings for them?

Fuck. What the hell had I done? I didn't know, and what was worse, I wasn't sure I could fix it.

CHAPTER 4
MITCH

"That was fucked up." I pushed my toes into a skate and leaned forward to pull it all the way onto my foot.

Jagger looked over at me like he had no idea what I was talking about. "You gonna elaborate?"

"The thing with Eden this morning," I said slowly, as though I thought he was dense for not knowing what I was referring to.

He knew, and we both knew it, but I couldn't resist the chance to get under his skin. He was too easy to rile up, some days.

"What about it?" he asked flatly. He didn't meet my eyes, instead busying himself with laces that were already tied and double knotted.

"You running off like that," I said. "What was that?" I crossed my arms over my chest and looked down my wide nose at him.

Watching him take off ahead of us, this morning, I

didn't know what to do or say. At the time, I had to let it go, but now... Now I needed to confront him about it. I needed to know what was going on in his head.

"That was me exercising," he said tersely. "What the fuck did you think it was?" He gave up on his laces and started to adjust his padding. Padding that didn't seem to need any adjustment.

"You being a coward," I said. "The moment you understood what Eden was saying, you bolted for the hills." I mimed running away with my pointer and middle finger.

He straightened up and scowled at me. "I saw no hills, dumbass."

I mimicked his tone. "I didn't mean it literally, *dumbass*. You said you needed time to think, but I saw the whites of your eyes before you ran." I hadn't, but close enough.

"You're full of shit. I meant what I said. I needed time to think. You pressuring me is not going to help." His dark brown eyes were darker with annoyance.

I preferred when they were darker with lust. In spite of his visible anger, my cock throbbed. It always did when I was close to him, or to Eden. When I was around both of them, I was permanently hard. Some days, I was so aroused by them, I thought my balls might drop off from the weight. I couldn't get enough of either of them.

"What is there to think about?" I asked. "Eden is incredible and we both know it. Do you really want her to walk away from you? From us? Because I don't. What we have, the three of us, is something unique and special. It went past being fuck buddies a long time ago."

I pointed my finger at him when he opened his mouth to deny that claim. "Don't tell me it didn't, because you know that would be a load of shit."

He got that 'I'm about to chew rocks and spit them out' look on his face. The one he always had when he was backed into a corner.

"So what if it did?" He grabbed up his stick and started to wind tape around it, more aggressive than was technically necessary. Better that than hitting me over the head with it, which, frankly, he looked tempted to do.

He was violent on and off the ice, but never toward me. Partly because I was at least as big as he was. He'd have to work hard to kick my ass.

"That doesn't mean we have to run off and get married."

I shoved my shoulder into his. "Who said anything about getting married? All she asked was for us to go out together and see where things go. We've both taken bigger risks on the ice."

When he didn't answer, I said, "That's what you're afraid of, isn't it? Taking a risk with her, in case it doesn't pay off."

"What happens if it doesn't?" He broke off the tape and smoothed down the end with the pad of his thumb.

"What then? We both know things won't go back to the way they were. Things never do. We get one shot at goal and if we miss, we're out."

"So you'd rather walk away than take that chance?" I picked up the tape when he set it aside and started on my own stick.

"No harm to anyone if I do," he said. He stood and grabbed up his helmet. "Might save you some hassle."

I frowned at him before I finished taping my stick and tossed the roll of tape to Cole Davis.

"Is this about Eden, or do you not want to be with me?"

I won't lie, that fucking stung. Jagger was my teammate, my best friend and my lover. I didn't want to lose any of that, much less all of it. Not to mention that playing together would be difficult if we ended it. One of us would end up transferring out for the sake of the team. Or we'd be thrown out on our asses, because without doubt, our performances would be negatively impacted.

Mine would anyway. Jagger would probably spend more time on the bench after slamming opposition players into the boards to let off steam. That was one of his favourite activities to begin with.

"I don't—" Jagger cut himself off with a click of his teeth. "This isn't about you."

"The hell it isn't," I snapped. "This is about you, me and Eden." My voice was getting louder. A couple of the guys had stopped to stare.

Cruz Brewer sauntered over like he owned the locker room. "As one of Cat's partners, I feel it's my duty to tell you that if either of you hurt Eden, I'll be obliged to shove a puck down your throat." He smiled threateningly.

"Fuck off, Brewer," Jagger snarled. "This is none of your business."

Cruz was unfazed. "I'll make it my business. And Easton, Shaw, Toby and Cole will too. Right guys?"

"Only if Cat is upset," Shaw Moss said. "Otherwise I'm staying the hell out of it."

"I can make it my business," Easton Grant agreed.

"Me too," Toby Glover said in his American drawl. "I like Eden, she's cool."

Cole said nothing, instead keeping his head down over his stick.

"I have no intention of hurting Eden." I gave Jagger the side eye.

What would I do if he decided he was done? With me or with Eden? Would Eden and I work without him? Would we want to? Frankly, I didn't want to find out. I meant what I said when I told her I was willing to give this a try, but I wanted to be with them both. I wasn't ready to contemplate anything else.

"Are you guys here to train, or for a social gathering?" Kage Foster called out from the doorway that led out to the rink.

"Jagger is here for a social gathering," Cruz replied. "You know how much he loves people." He grinned when Jagger flipped him off. "See what I mean? He's all sunshine and rainbows all day long."

"You're an asshole," Jagger told him.

Cruz just grinned more broadly. "You wouldn't be the first person to tell me that, and you won't be the last. Not even today. In fact, the first thing I did this morning was look at my reflection in the mirror and say, 'Cruz, you're a magnificent asshole.'"

Jagger muttered something that sounded like, "You're a fucking idiot," before walking on his skates toward the rink.

"You really did that?" Easton asked Cruz.

Cruz chuckled and patted Easton on his padded shoulder. "No, but tomorrow I will. Or better yet, you can say it for me." They headed out to the ice together, followed by Shaw who was shaking his head.

I watched them step out of the locker room with some measure of envy. Their relationship with Cat, and each other, were life goals, as far as I was concerned. They seemed to have everything together. Whereas my relationships seemed to be falling apart.

"I didn't mean to overhear," Cole said softly. "You can tell me to mind my own business if you want, but I get where you're coming from. When I first got together with Marley, Toby and Oliver, things were rocky and difficult. For a long time, I thought there was no way we would make it work." He glanced down at the floor. "I didn't think I was good enough to be with them. But Toby and Marley, they never gave up on me. And then, when it counted, I didn't give up on us either." He looked back up.

"You think Jagger doesn't think he's good enough?" I guessed. Only a couple of days ago, he was buried balls deep in my ass. I didn't do that with just anyone. Had I told him that though? I supposed I hadn't.

"If you want it to work, you have to communicate," Cole said. "You can't keep secrets, not even small ones. Definitely not big ones. All they do is eat away at you. They'll tear you apart at the seams. I know how hard it is to talk about your feelings and shit, but you have to. You just…" He shrugged. "You just do."

"Do you think I was too harsh on Jagger?" I asked. "He asked for time to think. I guess that's not unreasonable."

"Give him time," Cole said. "But let him know you're there when he's ready to talk. And maybe don't let him stew for too long."

"Right." Jagger would get himself worked up if I let him. Then the chances were, everything would go to hell. Once they'd slid down that slippery slope, coming back would be harder.

"Thanks." I gave him a playful punch on the bicep as we followed the rest of the team out to the ice.

"So…" I wrapped a towel around my waist and tucked in the side. I ran a hand through my damp hair to straighten it, before shaking it out. I liked it when it dried with that freshly fucked look.

"Save it," Jagger snapped. He rubbed the towel over his hair for about three seconds, tossed it aside and stomped over to his locker to pull out a pair of black boxer briefs.

"Chill out," I said. I followed him over and leaned my shoulder against the locker beside his. "I just wanted to say if you need some time, I'll give you time."

He barely glanced at me. "I do need it. That's why I fucking asked for it. This isn't a game, Mitch."

"I didn't think it was." I was tempted to step back from his anger, but I held my ground. "That's the point. This is important to me." I wanted to say he and Eden were important to me, but the words wouldn't come. Maybe he wasn't the only one who needed a bit of time. I might need some myself. If there was anything I was good at, it was jumping in with both feet and regretting it later.

Or sometimes, not regretting it later.

Either way, I was impulsive and maybe I shouldn't be. If there was any chance rushing in too fast got Eden or Jagger hurt, it wouldn't be worth it.

"You're right," I conceded. "We should take our time and move forward slowly. What's the rush?"

"Exactly," he said. "There's no fucking rush." He dragged a T-shirt over his head and stepped into a pair of grey track pants.

"Yeah." What more was there to say? He turned his

back to me, pulled on his hoodie, then sat down to put on socks and shoes.

I stared at his hunched form for a while before I pushed myself off the locker and walked over to mine to get dressed. I felt as though someone had thrown a bomb in the middle of me, Jagger and Eden, and this was the fallout from it. Honestly, this might only be the beginning of the explosion.

In pushing Jagger, I might have pushed him away. In turn, that might drive Eden away from us both.

The problem was, what the fuck did I do about it?

CHAPTER 5
EDEN

I tossed my keys and phone on the plush, blue and white armchair that sat largely unused beside the couch in the centre of the living room. Since no one used it regularly, it became a dumping ground for all sorts of crap. Mostly unopened catalogues and empty chocolate wrappers. Once in a while, Brock or I would get annoyed and clean it up. That time was coming, but it wasn't today. Today, I barely noticed it.

I headed to the kitchen to make myself a coffee and a snack. I was craving something sweet to balance the bitter taste in my mouth that lingered after my conversation with Mitch and Jagger.

I peeled open a banana before smearing one end of it in Nutella.

It was mostly healthy. Sort of.

I was in the middle of taking the first bite when Brock stepped through the back door.

He stopped to look at me, banana held in my hand, the other end halfway down my throat.

His eyebrows twitched.

I took a bite and tried not to choke.

He watched with a smile as I chewed and swallowed. "That looks tasty."

I didn't think he was referring to the banana.

"It is," I said, my voice higher than usual.

Don't think about smearing Nutella on his cock and sucking it off, I told myself. Of course, that was immediately the next thing in my brain.

"Don't let me stop you." He made himself a coffee and leaned against the kitchen counter to watch me eat.

I should have gobbled down the banana and headed in to have a shower before starting dinner. Instead, I locked my eyes on his and slid my mouth down the banana before taking a slow bite.

Both of his eyebrows rose. The front of his pants tented.

"Eden…" His voice was as strained as his seams.

My face heated. What the fuck was I thinking? Once again, I reminded myself he was my mother's ex. I shouldn't be trying to provoke him. We should make boundaries and stick to them.

"I'm sorry," I said quickly. "I got carried away." I stuffed the rest of the banana in my mouth and washed it down with coffee that was already half cold.

"Don't apologise." With tantalising slowness, he put down his mug and stepped closer. Eyes dark, he placed his hands on the countertop to either side of me, boxing me in.

"Don't ever apologise for being yourself. You're a beautiful, sexy woman. There's no reason why you shouldn't express that."

His body was warm against mine, his growing erection pressed against my hip. He was so close his breath brushed the side of my face.

I swallowed deeply. "We shouldn't…" My brain seemed to have short-circuited. The words that should define what we shouldn't do wouldn't come. What might come, was me. His proximity made me hot and wet.

He slid his knuckles down my cheek. "Do I have to remind you I'm not married to your mother anymore? Or anyone else."

"You were," I managed to squeak out. "You were my stepfather. That's… It's…" I shook my head. "We shouldn't."

"Because you don't want to?" he asked, his voice deep and husky, raising goosebumps all over my skin.

"It's not that simple. What would Mum think?" She'd lose her mind if she saw us like this.

Brock grabbed my wrists and pulled them up above my head. With one hand, he held them there, pressed against the cabinet behind me. "It's exactly that simple. I don't give a shit what Paula thinks anymore. I haven't for a long time. Our relationship ended years before the divorce. She moved on. I want to do the same."

My breath came more rapidly now. I wanted to wrap my legs around his waist and let him fuck me right here in the kitchen. I wanted to feel his cock buried deep inside me. I wanted him to pound into me like he hated me.

"You *should* move on," I finally said. "You deserve to be happy."

He snorted softly before letting my wrists go and stepping back. "I don't know about that."

I was torn between relief, and the urge to tell him to finish what he started.

I lowered my trembling hands, but stayed pressed against the countertop. There was more to consider here than my mother, and my former designation as his stepdaughter. I needed to work things out with Jagger and Mitch first. If it was over between us, I might jump in and fuck Brock. But they weren't, not yet, and I didn't want to go behind their backs.

As far as I'd been able to tell, my mother cheated on Brock. That was one of the reasons they separated. I wasn't going to cheat on them with him. That would make me as bad as her.

"Of course you deserve to be happy," I said. "Why wouldn't you?"

He turned away for a few moments and rubbed a hand over the back of his head.

When he turned back, his eyes were closed. He opened them, seemingly taking me in. Looking at me like I meant something more to him than a former stepdaughter and current housemate.

"Because when I was fucking your mother, I was thinking about you," he said, soft but frank. "I cared about her, but you were always the one I wanted."

I gaped at him for what felt like the longest time. "Me?" The word came out in a squeak. I cleared my throat and tried again. "Me?"

He smiled softly. "Yes, you. Why not you? You're fucking gorgeous, smart. You're… everything. The moment I met you, I was gone. I figured if I couldn't have you, at least I could be near you. So I married your mother. It was never going to work. My heart and balls only wanted you."

Before I could even respond to that, he turned and headed out of the kitchen.

His words echoed in my mind while I slipped into my room and out of my clothes. All this time, he wanted me? I was the one he cared about?

I'd be lying if I said I wasn't attracted to him back then too, but when he married my mother, that seemed to be that. There was no way in hell I would have started anything with him while he was with her. But now…

I turned on the water in the shower until it was warm enough to stand under. A cold shower would stimulate my blood more, so a hot one should settle me down, right?

And yet, I found myself taking the handheld shower wand out of its bracket and running it up and down the front of my body. Everywhere the spray touched tingled, like dozens of tiny fingers caressing my skin.

I held the shower head over my nipple, then the other, imagining Mitch and Jagger with their hands or mouths on me. I moved the water down over my belly slowly, like a lover taking his time to appreciate every centimetre of me.

I tried not to think it, but I imagined Brock on his knees in front of me, his big hands running up and down, touching me everywhere, learning every part of me.

When I stood with my legs apart and sprayed the water right onto my pussy, it was his hands, his mouth there instead. Teasing me with his fingers and tongue.

I leaned back against the shower wall and let the spray hit my pussy until my clit tingled and ached for more. I moved the water around slowly, teasing myself, allowing my mind to wander wherever it wanted to go. Right now, it was imagining Brock pressing me hard against the tiles, raising one of my legs and pushing his cock deep inside me.

I shivered, and rolled my hips as I moved the water rhythmically, simulating his touch on my most sensitive places.

I ran my other hand up my stomach and over my breast, to palm and pinch my nipple.

My eyes closed, I imagined it was Mitch's hand there, and Brock's mouth between my legs. Jagger was behind Mitch, thrusting into his ass. All three of them watched me with dark, intense eyes. Waiting for me to come for them. Silently insisting.

I bit my lip to hold back a moan, but I couldn't keep a second from slipping out and echoing around the bathroom. Had Brock heard? Part of me was unnerved by the thought, but mostly… Mostly, I wanted him to hear. Let him know what his words did to me. That I was thinking of him fucking me.

I moved the water faster, holding it close to my clit, almost too close for comfort. The water was slightly too hot. And perfect at the same time. It was as hot as my blood right now. Hotter.

I pinched my nipple harder, wanting to come, but wanting to draw it out at the same time.

Finally, I couldn't hold back any more. I came with a rush and a loud gasp, rocking against the water as it drove me into bliss that was sweet, if not the dizzying highs I experienced when I was with my lovers. This would only keep me satisfied for so long before I needed more. Wanted more.

I relaxed back against the wall, letting my pulse slow before I popped the wand back into its bracket and finished getting clean.

CHAPTER 6
EDEN

"He said *what?*" Marley whispered. "Holy crap." She stared at me, her lips apart in disbelief.

"Those were basically my thoughts too," I admitted. "I don't know what to think. Or what to say, for that matter."

I sat on the corner of her desk and rubbed my eyes. I'd barely slept for the last two nights. I was tired. Beyond tired.

Since our conversation, Brock and I had danced around each other, barely speaking.

I hadn't seen Mitch or Jagger. The only contact I had with either of them was a conversation via text, that consisted of random, and sometimes funny, gifs. For some reason, Mitch's mostly consisted of ducks, doing various duckish things. I wasn't sure if he was trying to be cute, or tell me something so obscure I couldn't figure it out.

Maybe it was his way of saying they were ducking me on purpose. If that was the case, I wish they'd come out and say it.

I was starting to feel like somebody threw all the parts of my life into a pot and were stirring vigourously. Could I grab the spoon and toss it out the window?

"Do you think your mother knows?" Marley asked. Her eyes were wide, the implication of Brock's admission turning the cogs and wheels in her mind.

I made a face that matched the churning in my stomach. "I don't know. I mean, she might have suspected he wasn't as into her as she was into him, but she might not have known why. If she did, wouldn't she have insisted I stay away from him?"

"She could have tried to insist *he* stay away from *you*," Marley suggested. "In which case, he clearly didn't listen. He was quick enough to let you stay in the house when she left." It seemed as though she wasn't sure who to judge in this scenario, if anyone.

"I thought he was being nice," I said. Was that naive of me? He'd always treated me with respect. If not as a father figure, then at least as a friend. It was…comfortable.

"I mean, I think of it as my home too. It never occurred to me there was anything to it. It's convenient to work and close to you and Cat. It never crossed my mind he was thinking something else."

"Are you sure?" she asked gently. "What about you? You never thought of him as the hot stepfather?"

My face heated when she hit the nail squarely on the head. I winced before admitting, "I did think of him that way. I mean, he's hot. But…"

I tossed around the thoughts in my mind, looking for the right words.

Finally, I exhaled out my nose and said, "I thought of him the way we might think of a movie star or someone like that, you know? Hot, but completely out of reach."

Plenty of times, I'd fantasised about what it would be like if he touched me, just like I had in the shower after that conversation. But I'd put it down to just that, a fantasy. A silly crush.

"And now he's not out of reach?" Marley asked. "Speaking as a woman who has no regrets about getting involved with someone some people considered to be out of bounds, I support you, whatever you do." She nodded over to the closed door to the treatment room. Inside, Oliver, her boss and boyfriend, was seeing a patient. They'd had a relationship long before Cat knew about it, much less approved of it. Things weren't always smooth sailing, but they'd come out the other end stronger than ever. Committed and deeply in love. Hashtag relationship goals.

"You think I should go for it?" I asked tentatively. With everything else going on right now, I hadn't really considered taking things further with Brock. Fantasised yes, definitely. Given it *serious* consideration, no.

Before she could respond, I said, "It's not even that

easy. I still don't know what's going on with Mitch or Jagger. I'm not sure I know which way is up. Everything is so *frustrating* right now." I needed a crystal ball to peek into the future and see how things turned out. Or not, because I might not like what I saw.

"What is your clit telling you to do?" Marley asked.

"Shouldn't you be asking what my heart is saying?" I asked.

She grinned. "There's no reason we can't think with both. After all, sex is important in a relationship. Falling in love is all very well, but if they can't get us off…"

I snorted softly. "I suppose so." I was usually the one giving my friends this kind of advice. Being on the receiving end was both new and strange. It was welcome though. I was never short on friends to confide in, even if Cat and Marley were both busy. They always made time to listen when I needed them. I was lucky to have them both as my besties.

"So?" she prompted.

"I think my clit is telling me to go back in time and not tell Jagger or Mitch what I was thinking," I admitted. "She's also telling me to let Brock fuck me senseless. I'm starting to think she can't be trusted."

Marley laughed sympathetically. "Okay, what is your heart telling you?"

I pushed my hair back off my forehead and scratched my ear. "Basically the same thing. But my brain is saying we can't go back, and I'm scared of what my mother might think. If she knows Brock's interest was with someone else, and I get together with him, she's going to put two and two together. What if she ends up hating me because of it?"

That idea made my heart ache. We didn't always get along, but she was still my mother. I loved her, even when she was at her most difficult and high-strung. Granted, that was a lot of the time, but what parent was perfect? What daughter, for that matter?

"I went through the exact same thought process with Oliver," Marley said. "I was scared Cat would hate me. I was scared you'd hate me too, but you were there for me when no one else was. And she eventually understood."

"I'd always be there for you," I assured her. "And Cat is too good a friend to turn her back on you for long. Besides, she'd know that would have upset Oliver. Both of them have always been close. She wouldn't jeopardise that for her own pride."

"But you think your mother would?" Marley asked. "I know we speculated before that she cheated. If she did, she made her choice long before any of this. And she seems happy with her new partner anyway. If Brock wasn't into you, she wouldn't have found… What's his name?"

"John," I said. "According to Mum, he's a businessman. The total opposite of her." My mother was an artist who floated through life with a smile on her lips and paint on the tip of her nose. She was spontaneous, and flaky as fuck.

"Sounds like the perfect match," Marley said. "Honestly, I can't see your mother hating you anyway. She's too— What's the word?"

"I think it's three words," I said. "Gives-no-fucks. Maybe, but at the end of the day she's human like the rest of us. She could decide she wants to scratch his eyes out, and she might also turn around and give us her blessing. It depends which way the wind is blowing."

"There's your answer," Marley said with a snap of her fingers. "Figure out which way the wind is blowing before you tell her. Then drop everything and get ready to be hugged, or run like hell."

I choked back a laugh. "I'll keep that in mind. First, I need to know what the hell is going on with Mitch and Jagger. I'm starting to feel like I need a couple name for them. Magger or Jitch. Or maybe based on their last names, Sanderson and Ward."

"Wanderson or Sard." Marley giggled. "Or you could use all of them on rotation. Depending on which you're feeling at the time."

I laughed and shook my head at her. "Either way, I need to sort things out with them before I even *think* about jumping into anything else. I mean, they might decide they want to take things further with me, but don't want Brock in the picture."

A dull headache started to thump at the inside of my head. I rubbed my temples slowly, trying to ease it away.

"Or vice versa," Marley said. "When getting involved with multiple partners, they have to get along with each other. Otherwise, you're going to feel like a mother mediating toddler battles. Mine got off to a rocky start, but they get along like brothers now. Thank fuck." She made a face.

I gathered the same about Cat's boyfriends. It certainly would be easier if they liked each other. Or more than liked each other, like Jagger and Mitch. I'd never been jealous of their friendship and I wouldn't be jealous if that went further. Love was love, after all. I was all for them exploring their relationship and taking it to the next level.

"What are you going to do about them?" Marley asked.

"I don't know," I admitted. "I don't want to look like I'm desperate. I want to give them space, but I feel like the longer it goes before I see them again, the more difficult it'll be to move forward. Like… Out of sight out of mind."

"You think if they don't see you soon, they'll forget you exist?" Marley teased gently.

"Something like that," I agreed reluctantly. "You've seen the kind of women that surround the team when the guys go out anywhere. Compared to them, I'm not exactly memorable."

Marley placed her hands on the armrests of her chair, pushed herself to her feet and came around to stand in front of me. "Eden Wright, don't you dare say things like that about my best friend. You are *very* memorable, I promise you that. If they'd forget you for some one night stand, they don't deserve you. I'm starting to think I should go and kick them in the balls on your behalf."

"I don't think we're quite at that point yet," I said, snort-laughing. "But I appreciate you. You've always had my back when I wasn't sure anyone else did."

I was close to Cat now, but she'd moved to Melbourne for several years. I didn't really get to know her until she returned. She and Marley were best friends in school and picked up where they left off. Marley and I never stopped being close, and Cat slotted in like she never left.

"And you've always had mine," Marley said. "But please let me know if you get to that point. I'm only too happy to put on my pointy-toed heels and give them a good workout." She pushed her glasses back up her nose and grinned.

"You'll be the first to know," I assured her. "What do you think I should do? Should I try to pin them down?"

She gave me a sly smile. "I can do better than that." She reached for her phone.

CHAPTER 7
JAGGER

I slumped down in the stands. "This is bullshit."

Mitch glanced over at me. "Which part? The part where we have to interact with kids, or the part about being back at the skating rink where we used to train and play before we went pro? Or the part where you have to go out in public and be seen by actual people?"

"All of it," I said with a grunt. "I don't remember signing up to be a junior hockey coach."

"It's in the small print of your contract." Kage stopped in front of us. "Right under the bit where you agreed to be a role model for kids everywhere to look up to. In order to continue to expand, the AIHL wants to encourage participation and enthusiasm at a grass-roots level. That includes getting out of bed and doing things like this. If that interrupts your social calendar, too bad."

Any other time he would have said 'too fucking

bad,' his Canadian drawl making the words strangely hot. Today though, the rink was swarming with children aged between ten and fourteen. No doubt he didn't want to offend their sensitive little fucking ears. As if they didn't hear words like that at school. Hell, they probably said them more than I did.

I scowled at him. "I should have had my agent read my contract carefully. I would have insisted on leaving that part out."

We all knew there was no such clause in any of our contracts. It came under the umbrella of 'stuff the team expected us to do, for the good of the community and the sport as a whole.' Yeah, that was a mouthful.

It didn't mean I wasn't going to bitch about it once in a while though. Since Shaw got together with Cat, and lightened up slightly, someone had to be the grumpy asshole of the team. I'd delegated that role to myself. It was a comfortable fit, most of the time.

Mitch playfully punched me on the arm. "No you wouldn't. Even your grumpy ass enjoys this stuff as much as the rest of us do."

I punched him back, just as hard. "Says you."

He rubbed his arm and grinned. "Yeah, says me. Because you know it's true. You want those kids to idolise you." He jerked his thumb towards the closest of them.

They were watching us, while pretending not to watch us. If any of them looked at us straight on, it was usually with wide eyes and hero worship-like admiration. Exactly how kid-Jagger would have looked at people like me.

If they knew the real me, they'd idolise somebody else, someone more deserving. Someone like Mitch or Kage.

"You're projecting," I told him. "You want them to idolise *you*. You want them to think you're a good guy." Which he was. He was a much better person than I would ever be.

If he could, he'd be here at the rink with the kids every day, helping them to become the best versions of themselves. Sometimes I wondered if I was another of his projects. Maybe, deep down, he thought he could make me into something, someone, better than I was.

I didn't like his chances. Sooner or later, he was going to figure out I was a lost cause.

"I don't care what they think of me, as long as they support the Ghouls." Most of Opal Springs supported us. The construction of our arena was a huge boost to the economy. It had created hundreds of jobs and continued to do so as the town grew.

That growth was a bonus, on top of the fact we played the best sport in the world, and one of the fastest growing in Australia.

Of course, some people bitched that Opal Springs was getting too big, but you couldn't please everyone. Those who did were usually shot down—verbally—by the rest of the town. Mostly, we saved the violence for the ice.

He shook his head, undeterred. "You're so full of it. Right, Coach?" He glanced over at Kage.

"He's full of something all right," Kage said. His Canadian accent was more pronounced when he spoke slowly, derisively. "He's as grumpy as a pissed off moose."

"I'd flip you off, but I have more class than that," I said. "In my head, I'm sticking up two middle fingers at both of you." I smirked at them.

"You're not flipping us off because there are children present," Kage said. "Whether you want to admit it or not, you care about them and your reputation. Especially since your reputation is important to your inclusion on the team." He returned my smirk.

"Threatening people is not classy," I remarked. "Especially when they happen to be the best centre in the league."

"I don't know," Mitch said slowly, "Coast Riggs is pretty good. I'm not too shabby either."

I looked at him evenly. I stood by what I said. I was good at my job and I'd own every bit of it. I didn't give a fuck what anyone else thought, not even Mitch. Not even Eden. Not when it came to my skills on the ice.

They could question everything else about me and I wouldn't give a shit. This was the one thing I was good at. The one thing I was proud of. The hill I'd ultimately die on if I had to. Which I wouldn't, because I had money in the bank to back up my claim. This was the Ghouls' season to smash all the other teams. We weren't new anymore. It was time for us to dominate.

Dominating made me think of Eden lying spread in front of Mitch and me, taking his cock while I rammed into him.

My balls were instantly heavier. I hadn't seen or texted her for days. I was currently trying to convince myself and my cock that I didn't miss her. I'd kept Mitch at arm's length and was also trying to convince myself I didn't miss him either.

How was that going for me? Not so great, if I'm honest.

All my life, I'd tried to avoid complicated situations. After I finished school, I became a tiler. Tiles didn't argue with you, they just let you lay them, and cut them. The rest of my time, I played hockey, and fucked by the hour. At the end of the night, I went home alone to enjoy my own space. Everything was easy.

Now, nothing was easy. I felt as though I hit a puck square into the centre of the basket, but somehow the fucking thing got tangled in the net. I couldn't just whack it with a stick and smash it loose. Now it was stuck, I had two options: walk away, or get tangled up with it.

I didn't like either fucking option.

"Get your skates on and get out there." Kage jerked his head towards the ice. "Be a role model, not a dickhead." Evidently, he was done with being nice.

"Yes, Coach," Mitch said cheerfully. Did he always

have to be so fucking happy? He was like a sunny day when you really wanted rain and storm clouds. Usually, I liked that about him, but today it was rubbing me the wrong way.

I couldn't take things in my stride the way he did. I didn't want to. I wanted to skate at my own pace. What was wrong with that? Nothing, that's what. If there was, too fucking bad. This was who I was. Who I'd always be.

Kage looked at me, one eyebrow raised until I nodded.

"Got it," I said simply. I leaned over and started to pull on my skates.

The asshole actually waited until I was lacing them up before he moved on to annoy the shit out of someone else. Don't get me wrong, he was a fucking good coach, but I didn't need him busting my ass. I already had Mitch for that.

Also, I hadn't missed seeing him checking out Eden when he thought no one was looking. He might take the situation as permission to move in on her, if we weren't careful. What would it mean if he did? I'd pushed her away, but she was still my woman. If he hurt her, I'd break his face. When it came to her, I wouldn't rule out violence, wherever it may occur.

I checked my laces, and glanced over to Mitch. He was bent over his own skates, toned body in the usual track pants and Ghouls hoodie. The way it felt to be buried inside him flooded into my brain and body, making my cock harder. I wasn't going to compare fucking him to fucking Eden. My cock loved them both equally. He didn't care who he was inside, as long as it was warm and tight.

I should start to think more with my head and less with my dick.

"I know what you're thinking," Mitch said without looking around. "You're wishing Eden was here so we could slip off to the locker rooms for a quick fuck."

That was what I was thinking *now*. The asshole knew just what to say to get straight into my brain. And straight to my cock.

"You're projecting again," I said.

He glanced over at me and grinned. I tried to ignore the way my heart flipped, but resisting my attraction to him was virtually impossible. As impossible as resisting my attraction to Eden.

So, why was I trying to resist? Apart from making my life complicated, that was. No, there was more to it than that. No way in the world was I going to admit I was scared of commitment, or getting hurt. Fuck that.

No, I told myself I liked my life as it was and didn't need or want it to change. If we weren't training, we were playing and if we weren't playing, we were travelling to games. And if we weren't doing that, we were doing interviews and grassroots training days for kids, like this.

When was I supposed to fit in a relationship?

I glanced over at Cruz, when he laughed so loud it almost echoed through the rink.

He stood on the edge, his arm draped over Easton's shoulders, relaxed and comfortable. Even Shaw, who stood a couple of metres away, was almost smiling. At the same time, he was shaking his head at them.

Toby and Cole stood on the other side of the rink. Toby was talking; his hands moved as he seemed to be describing something. Cole nodded every so often, and smiled now and again, while keeping an eye on everything around him.

It seemed like everyone around me had their shit together. With each other.

Could I do that too? Did I want to? What was the alternative? Mitch and Eden would be done with me if I turned my back on them. I wouldn't blame them. I'd be done with me too. Maybe they were better off without me. They'd be cute together.

Although, even if I was inclined to give people couple names, I didn't know what the hell theirs would be. Meden or Eitch? Neither had a ring to them. The first sounded like some weird Greek monster. The kind with snakes for hair. The second sounded like the symptom of some nasty rash. I wanted to scratch just thinking about it.

"I'm not projecting, I'm saying we have the same taste in hobbies," Mitch said. "Especially fuc— being intimate."

I eyed him. "I suppose we do. What are you going to do if I don't want in?"

I didn't need to explain what I was referring to. We both understood.

He shrugged. "Keep trying to convince you to change your mind, I guess."

"And if I won't?" I asked.

"Then I'll keep trying harder, harder, harder," he said rhythmically. He even moved his hips in time to his words.

Fuck.

"Stop that," I snapped. "The kids don't need to see me with a boner."

He grinned. "Not sorry."

"I'm shocked," I said sarcastically. "You're such a—" I stopped short as a familiar head of purple hair appeared in the corner of my eye.

What the hell was Eden doing here?

CHAPTER 8
EDEN

"I don't know about this," I said under my breath.

"Relax," Cat said easily. "The rink is open to the public, we have every right to be here. Besides, I want to see my guys with the kids. They love doing stuff like this." She saw the expression on my face and smiled. "I know, if anyone said that about them a couple of years ago, I wouldn't have believed it either. But they really do enjoy giving back to the community."

"I believe you." I held my hands up in surrender. "Most of the team does."

Except Jagger, who was scowling when I caught sight of him sitting in the stands. I watched him and Mitch talk for a couple of minutes before they realised I was here. Mitch looked happy to see me. Jagger, not so much.

"Toby is in his element here," Marley said. She

nodded over to where he crouched in front of a group of awestruck kids.

I couldn't hear what he was saying, but they hung on every word, nodding and laughing.

"He's a big kid himself," she added with a grin.

"Aren't they all?" Cat rolled her eyes playfully.

I couldn't argue with that. It was one of the things I liked about Mitch and Jagger. In spite of Jagger's grumpy exterior, he had his lighter moments. I treasured each one of them. I missed them.

"Let's sit down," Marley said.

I followed her and Cat to the stands, sitting where the guys recently vacated. They were now down on the ice, teaching the kids how to hold a stick, hit a puck, and in some cases, stay upright on ice skates.

Mitch was grinning and laughing with a group of ten-year-old kids.

Jagger stood nearby, scowling like he wished he was anywhere but here. Still, he was quick to grab a girl with blonde pigtails, right before her feet slid out from under her.

Once she regained her balance, he stepped back and resumed scowling.

"Looks like Toby might have some competition for his job," Marley remarked.

Toby knelt in front of the goal, a girl with short red hair beside him. She had full goalie protective gear on, including a mask over her face. Her body was tense with concentration as the other kids hit the puck toward the goal. She saved one with her stick and another with her gloved hand. Her reflexes and skills were amazing for a kid that young. Toby was grinning the whole time, encouraging her, and giving her tips.

"Future AWIHL for sure," I agreed. Hopefully, by the time she was old enough, the women's league would be established, and players, regardless of gender, were making as much money as those in North America.

A man from the local newspaper was moving around the rink, taking photos. He took a lot of Toby and his little protégé.

"Looks like everyone is having a good time." Kage Foster stopped beside us to look out over the rink. He turned and let his gaze linger on me.

"I'm going to get a coffee," Marley declared. She pushed herself to her feet.

"I'll come with you," Cat said. To me she added, "We'll bring you back one." She gave me a meaningful look of encouragement before they both hurried away.

Yeah, they were about as subtle as a flamingo on stilts, waving a rainbow flag.

I nodded my thanks and leaned back to watch the guys, half an eye on Kage.

"Most of them," I agreed, responding to Kage. My gaze slid back to Jagger, who was hitting pucks back to Mitch, and the handful of kids he was working with.

He glanced over at me and his expression tightened.

I offered him a smile, but he glanced away before a puck slid past him.

"He's laughing on the inside," Kage offered.

I snorted. "He's keeping it well-hidden."

The team's head coach had seen us together often enough to know I was involved with both guys. They respected him and so did I. It didn't hurt that he was handsome, in a rugged sort of way. Like Brock, silver was sprinkled through his hair, here and there.

"Jagger isn't the sort of guy to lay it all on the table," Kage agreed. "Not like Mitch. He's the kind to bare it all, and then some." He gave me a searching look, like he was trying to figure out where we all fit together.

"He really is." I nodded. Most of it, anyway. I still had no idea where I stood with either of them. I hadn't expected a welcome party, but scowls and vague smiles were all I got.

"What about you?" I asked. If they weren't going to give me anything, then maybe I could give them something to think about. I started with a bright smile for Kage, and cocked my head as I waited for him to answer. "Are you a closed book or an open book?"

He looked surprised at the question, but his expression became thoughtful. "I like to think I'm the kind of book a person can get into, but that leaves them guessing at just the right places. Keeps them wanting more."

His expression was mild, but his words had me blushing.

"So you're a mystery novel," I said.

"That sounds about right," he said. "The kind you enjoy when you're curled up in bed." Faint lines around his eyes crinkled as he smiled. "What about you?"

I leaned forward. "I'm the kind of smutty romance you read with one hand."

His eyes widened and he grinned. "Is that so?"

"Definitely," I agreed. "Maybe we should explore that sometime."

His brow dipped. "Aren't you and—" He jerked his head towards the rink.

I sighed. "I don't know what we are." I briefly told him about the situation, leaving out any mention of Brock.

"Sounds messy," he said.

"It is," I said. "I came here today to try to talk to them. I didn't know what else to do."

Kage sat in the chair beside me and crossed his legs. "I appreciate you being honest with me. Now it's my turn to be honest with you. I'm very tempted to suggest we disappear into the locker room so I can mess up your make-up and hair. One good fuck with me and you'd forget both of them."

Holy shit, that was blunt.

"You think so?" I asked lightly.

He looked over at me. Electricity crackled between us, hot and bright. I wouldn't have been surprised if it was visible to everyone in the rink.

"I know so. Unfortunately, there are kids present,

and they may walk in at exactly the wrong time. I'll make a note to hold these events at our arena next time. My office would have been perfect."

"Your office would have been perfect for what?" Jagger demanded.

I hadn't seen him approach, but now he was standing right in front of us.

I startled slightly, but Kage didn't so much as flinch.

"You're supposed to be on the ice, Sanderson," Kage said evenly.

"And let you make moves on my woman?" Jagger demanded. "What the f— Heck?" He was angry, but apparently not angry enough to forget he shouldn't swear in front of all those children.

I stared at him. "Your woman? Says who? You haven't spoken to me for days. How am I supposed to know what you're thinking or feeling?" His anger and possessiveness were hot, but they didn't clarify the situation. If anything, they left me more confused than ever.

"*I* didn't even know," he snapped. "Seeing you with him…" He gestured towards Kage and shook his head. "Is something going on between you?"

"Not yet, but if you don't get your head out of your ass, there might be," Kage said, still unruffled.

"How about I rearrange your face?" Jagger snarled. He started towards Kage, gloved hands curled into fists.

"How about you don't?" Mitch grabbed one of his arms and held him back. "What the hell is going on here?"

"Kage is trying to muscle in on our woman," Jagger said.

Mitch stared at him, then Kage, then at me.

"Do you want to be with Kage?" He seemed confused rather than hurt or angry.

I stared back at all three of them before rising to my feet and pointing at the two players. "I want you two to figure out what you want. If it's not me, then why shouldn't I go out with someone else? Why not Kage?"

Apart from being the mother of all complications, that might affect how they worked together. Right now, I couldn't bring myself to give a shit. If they didn't want me, then why shouldn't Kage fuck me senseless?

I started to step away.

"Wait," Mitch called out.

I stopped, but didn't look back. "What?"

"I want you," he said. "So does Jagger. Right Jag?"

I turned around slowly and locked my gaze on the dark-haired centre.

He pressed his lips together. "I want Eden, and Mitch," he ground out. "If you both want more than just, you know, s-e-x, then… I want to try and see how it goes. Maybe we have a future together and maybe we don't." Grudgingly and on a long sigh, he added, "I guess it wouldn't hurt to find out."

"But if you want Kage too, I support that," Mitch said hastily. He seemed desperate to cover all of the bases before I started to bolt for home. He glanced at the coach like the older man better not do anything to hurt me or he'd personally rip his arms off.

"We had one conversation," I said.

"You seemed to enjoy the conversation," Kage said. "I know I did. Look, we're all adults here. It seems to me like the three of you aren't completely committed. I want to take Eden out and get to know her. And you guys can do the same. Wherever all of this ends up, it ends up." He shrugged, but he hadn't flinched through the whole conversation. He was laying his cards out on the table, making his play. Take it or leave it. The openness was refreshing. If it helped Mitch and Jagger to figure their shit out, then all the better.

"Sounds reasonable to me," Mitch said with a hint of reluctance. "If that's what Eden wants."

"What if it goes beyond a date?" Jagger asked.

"If it does, then it does." Kage shrugged. "I say we let Eden decide what, and *who*, she does." He emphasised the word, drawing it out.

I sat back down slowly. "So, none of you mind if I see all of you?" I couldn't deny my attraction to Mitch or Jagger, or that I found Kage intriguing. This was a lot, but for once I didn't want to back down, or back away. I wanted to jump in with both feet and see where I landed. I was done staying back from the edge and not taking chances. Life was too fucking short not to take a leap once in a while.

"I don't mind," Mitch said. "Unless you choose Kage

over us. Then I'll mind." He gave Kage another dark look.

"Not my fault if I'm irresistible," Kage said with a grin.

Jagger snorted. He didn't seem convinced about this arrangement. One thing was clear, he had no intention of letting me go. He'd rather share me with Mitch and Kage, than not have me at all.

"There's something else," I said slowly. Keeping it as brief and PG as possible, I told them about Brock.

None of them seemed surprised, least of all Mitch or Jagger.

"I've seen the way he looks at you when he thinks no one else is looking," Mitch said. "He's as hot for you as I am."

"As we are," Jagger growled.

"As *we* are," Kage agreed, before staring Jagger down.

"Fuck." Jagger mouthed the word. "Where does this leave us?"

"Right where we were a couple of minutes ago," Mitch said. "Eden gets to decide what and who she does. Whether that's the three of us or Brock. Or the three of us *and* Brock. As long as we communicate with each other, I don't see why we can't make this work."

"Fine by me," Kage said with a shrug. "Eden, want to have dinner with me tonight?"

I glanced at the other two guys, before I nodded. "I'd love to."

"Eden, do you want to go out with Jagger and me on Friday night?" Mitch asked.

"I'd love to," I said again.

Jagger nodded along with me.

So much for not getting complicated. This just got all of that and more, and I was here for it. I hoped this didn't end badly for all of us.

CHAPTER 9
EDEN

"Going out?" Brock looked me up and down, taking in my short skirt and white boob tube that showed off a decent amount of cleavage.

"I have a date." I shrugged into a leather jacket and grabbed my bag. Kage said he'd pick me up. According to the clock on my phone, he'd be here in a couple of minutes, if he was on time. I suspected he was the punctual type, but time would tell. For all I knew, he'd turn up an hour late.

"With Mitch and Jagger?" Brock asked.

"No, I'm going out with Kage," I replied lightly.

Brock's eyes narrowed in surprise. "The Ghouls' coach? When did that happen?"

"This morning." Honestly, I wasn't sure how much to tell him. How exactly did someone broach the subject of dating multiple men? I still hadn't resolved the issue of

Brock being my former stepfather, much less confidante.

Welcome to Complicatedville. Population: me.

"I see." He nodded slowly, but his expression was guarded. "What about the other two?"

"I'm seeing them on Friday night," I replied, more easily than I felt. "We're all taking things casually for a while. You know, testing the waters."

"I see," he said again. He looked me straight in the eyes and took my bag out of my hand. He placed it down on the countertop and grabbed my wrists. He pushed me a couple of steps until my back was pressed against the wall.

"Are you going to fuck him?" His body was hard against mine.

I swallowed. "I don't know. Maybe."

"Maybe," he echoed. He pressed one hand to the wall beside my face and slipped the other down my hip and between my thighs. "You're going to let him fuck this?"

I gasped as he grazed his fingers across the gusset of my panties. "I don't know." I was wet as hell, my body throbbing for more. Without thinking, I moved my hips, rubbing my pussy against his hand.

"You like that, hmmm?" he said, his voice deep, husky. "You want me to touch you? You want me to get you off?"

I moaned softly. How should I respond to that? I decided to go with honesty.

"Yes."

That was all he needed. He yanked my panties aside and plunged two of his fingers straight into my wet heat.

I gasped at the suddenness of his penetration, but then I was riding his hand, his heel rubbing against my clit.

"Fuck," he whispered. "I've waited so long to touch your beautiful pussy. Too fucking long. This right here, you, your pussy, you belong to me. Mine. I don't care who else you fuck, as long as you don't forget you'll always be mine."

His words made me hotter and hotter, blood pounding through my body.

"Tonight, I fuck you with my hand," he said. "Next time I'm going to fuck you with my mouth. Then I'm going to pound my cock into your pussy like I've always fantasised about. On the kitchen counter, over the table, in my bed. On the couch, in the shower, everywhere. I'm going to fuck you every way I've dreamt of fucking you for all these years. And you're going to take everything I give you."

I groaned. "Yes. Yes, I want all of that." I wanted to live out every single one of his fantasies, however filthy they might be. I'd let him have me any way he wanted me. I was done holding back because of other people. It was time for me to live my life, and enjoy every moment of it, with every man who wanted me as much as I wanted them.

I pressed my hand between us and over the front of his jeans. His erection was thick and hard against the cotton fabric.

"Not yet." He pushed my hand away. "You'll get my cock when I'm ready to give it to you. I'm going to make you come. When you go on your date tonight, you'll still be wet from my hand. When he slides his cock into your pussy, you'll know it was me who made you so slick. Bring him back here, so I can hear him fuck you."

"Okay," I whispered. I was so close. Hovering right on the edge of the precipice, ready to jump all the way over.

He tugged down the front of my top and the cup of my bra and leaned down to suck my nipple between his lips. His teeth grazed my sensitive skin, making me moan again.

He worked me harder with his fingers, driving me closer and closer until I finally came, crying out and grinding myself against his hand.

"Fuck, yeah, that's my slut," he groaned. "That's it, doing exactly what I told you to do." He wrapped a hand around my throat. "That's what you're going to keep doing. What I tell you to do. Understood?"

I was quivering when I nodded.

"Out loud," he insisted.

"I understand," I managed to say. "I'm going to obey you."

"Yes, you are, because you're my slut." He squeezed

my throat more tightly before slipping his fingers out of me and pressing them between my lips. "Taste yourself."

I sucked my release from his fingers while my pulse finally started to slow down. His skin was salty and sweet at the same time. Warm, but rough.

"That's my girl," he said. "I'll be waiting for you to bring Kage home. You're going to spread your legs for him like the slut you are and scream out for me to hear."

"I will," I assured him. I wanted that.

I wanted it very much.

"You look a little flustered," Kage said when I answered the door. "Fucking gorgeous, but flustered."

"I'm excited," I said honestly. "Where are we going?"

He gave me a cagey look. "Wait and see. Do you trust me?"

I looked at him sideways, teasingly. "I don't know, should I?"

He grinned. "Definitely. I'm very trustworthy." He leaned over to graze his lips over my cheek, then took my hand and led me to his car, a dark blue Mercedes that looked relatively new.

I remembered he was a professional hockey player in Canada before he became a coach. He would have made a decent living up there.

He opened the passenger door for me and gestured for me to climb inside.

I gave him the obligatory, 'I can open my own door' glance, but nodded my thanks and sat, careful to give him a glimpse of my dark red G string.

His Adam's apple bobbed, and eyes widened before he closed the door behind me and stepped around to the driver's side.

We sang along—him well, me badly—to Wolf Venom, before we pulled up outside a small restaurant on the edge of town.

"Do you like Italian?" Kage asked.

"I love Italian," I said. "Pizza, pasta, gelato. What's not to love?"

"My thinking exactly." He hopped out and hurried around to open my door.

I gave him another reproachful glance before sliding out of the car and taking his arm.

"This place hasn't been open long, and I've been wanting to try it," he said.

"One of the best things about the Ghouls going pro, and the town growing, is the increase of amazing restaurants in Opal Springs," I said.

Inside the restaurant was toasty warm, a delicious contrast from the cold evening. Several tables were spread out across a wide room, each with a red tablecloth and a candle flickering in the centre.

"Very romantic," I said.

"I figured you deserved a bit of romance." He

nodded to the maître d', who led us to a table in the corner and handed us our menus.

"I don't know about deserved," I said. Thinking about Brock pressing me up against the door and calling me a slut, made me wonder if a quick hamburger might be more appropriate.

"Definitely deserved," Kage said. "A beautiful woman should have beautiful surroundings. And fine food."

"And pleasant company," I said.

He clicked his tongue. "Shame you're stuck with me then." His eyes shone with humour.

I laughed. "Who says you're not pleasant?"

"Usually, at the end of a long training session, the guys would agree that I'm not," he said. "And all of my exes." He leaned forward and said, "I try not to be too pleasant in the bedroom. It's not the place for politeness, if you know what I mean."

"I think I do," I agreed, my face flushed again. "As it happens, I've always preferred dirty to nice." After all, I was sitting here in damp panties.

"I knew you were my kind of woman," Kage said. "That's exactly what I like, too. I look forward to showing you." His eyes glowed in the light of the candle.

"I look forward to it too." I worried my lip with my teeth and scanned the menu. "Everything sounds so good. How am I supposed to choose?"

"Why choose?" he said lightly. "Let's pick a couple of

different things and share."

"You don't mind sharing?" I asked, not only referring to dinner.

"I'm the middle child of five," he said. "I could share before I could walk. Since I'm older now, I make a point of only sharing when it matters. Only the important, special things."

"Like Italian food," I said.

He laughed. "That too. Life is too short to miss out on the things you want." His gaze was firmly locked on me. "I have a confession to make. I was hoping you'd become available. I wasn't going to muscle in on Mitch and Jagger's territory, but I've been interested in you for a while. I saw you keeping your distance from them this morning and took that as an opportunity."

"Would you have preferred they weren't involved?" I asked, hoping for an honest answer.

He considered for a moment. "I'm man enough to admit that I wouldn't have minded having you to myself. But I can handle whatever situation gets thrown at us."

"We're an us already?" I asked.

He gave me a lopsided smile. "Sure we are. And if we aren't now, we will be soon. I'm not going to leave you waiting to find out how I feel. Like I told the guys, I want to get to know you. I want to see where this leads. And, yes, I want very much to fuck you."

"That's very forward of you," I said. "I appreciate that. I'm done with guessing. I want to know exactly where I stand." If he could give me that, then maybe something would grow from this.

"Then that's what you'll get from me," he said. "And if you ever feel like I'm not giving you enough, you only have to tell me. I'll come right out and fill you in. But I meant what I said in the rink. Once I fuck you, you'll never be able to forget me. I'm going to make you mine."

"You seem very sure of that," I said. My pulse was racing like a runaway train. The high-speed magnetic kind that travelled between cities in a matter of minutes.

"I know what I want and I go after it," he said. "Sometimes I have to wait for the right opportunity, but it comes along sooner or later. And for us, it did. I'm going to show you that, if you give me a chance." He didn't look like he was giving me much of a choice. His confidence was captivating.

I couldn't help asking, "What if I don't?" I cocked my head at him and gave him a challenging look. He was cocky, and I wasn't letting him get off too easily.

He pressed his lips together and rolled them a couple of times. "Then I'll have to work harder. No one has ever said I give up on something I want, because I don't. I haven't yet and I don't intend to start now."

"And, what happens if you decide you don't like me as much as you thought you would?" I asked. There was always that possibility. Wanting to fuck each other, and getting along in a committed relationship, were two different things. We might have nothing in common.

"Not gonna happen," he said with confidence. "I'm a good judge of character. Besides, I've always had a thing for women with purple hair."

"What if I change my hair colour?" I asked. "I might decide to go pink."

"I like pink too," he said. "And green, and blue, and natural. Whatever hair colour you choose, it'll look perfect wrapped around my fist."

CHAPTER 10
EDEN

"This was amazing." I licked my lips and swallowed the last of the lemon gelato.

"It absolutely was," he agreed. "The food wasn't bad either." He picked up a clean napkin and dabbed at the side of my mouth.

I sat still while he inspected my face, with one eyebrow raised in amusement.

"There." He put down the napkin and sat back. "Perfect." He picked up his almost empty wine glass and took a sip.

"You might have to roll me out the door." I patted my full stomach. I was going to need extra time in the gym tomorrow to work this meal off, but it was totally worth it. I'd never had meatballs that tender, and the truffle cream on the pasta was next level.

"I don't mind carrying you," Kage said. "Or better yet, helping you to work it off." One eyebrow twitched upward, along with that side of his mouth, his playful side on display.

I leaned forward and whispered. "I think if you bent me over the table here, people would notice."

"I don't care," he said, a smile hovering on the corners of his mouth. "Do you?"

"Opal Springs is growing, but it's still a small town," I said. "Gossip would get around in about ten seconds flat. I don't think I'm ready to be the subject of that." If that wasn't a consideration, I'd bend myself over and let him fuck me boneless.

"I guess we better go somewhere else then." He adjusted himself in his chair.

My tongue swiped over my bottom lip. "About that."

I needed to tell him everything, and I had no idea how he'd take it. He might decide my life was too screwed up for him to be a part of after all. Honestly, I wasn't sure I'd blame him. But I had to be upfront with him about this. Anything else would be dishonest.

His brow creased as he frowned. "I know we didn't make any promises…"

"No we didn't, but it's not about that," I said quickly. I made a face and started tentatively, briefly telling him what Brock insisted on.

Kage's eyes widened and darkened. "Let me get this straight. Your former stepfather, who you live with, who is into you, wants to hear me fuck you?"

"Basically, yes," I said. "If you're not into that, I understand. I mean, it is a bit—"

"I'm in," Kage said quickly. "I've never minded an audience. If he wants to listen, I'm down for it. Hell, if he wants to *watch*, I'm down for that too."

My pulse ratcheted up immediately. I didn't think Kage was shy, but I hadn't realised he was quite so outgoing. Although nerves fluttered through me, I was excited at the same time. I liked being the centre of attention between Jagger and Mitch. The idea of being in the middle of Brock and Kage was equally compelling.

"I guess we should get out of here then," I said. I reached for my card, but Kage was already on his feet, heading to pay for the meal.

"I'll get it next time," I said.

"That's negotiable," he said. "At least we can agree there'll be a next time." He placed a hand on my lower back and led me back to his car.

"This is your room, hmmm?" Kage looked around slowly.

I winced. "It could use an update. It hasn't been painted for a while."

Thank fuck it wasn't bright purple like the room I had when I was a kid. Back when it was just Mum and me, I saturated my entire world in the colour. Now, I just had purple hair and a purple car. With lavender bedcovers. I might also own a couple of pairs of purple boots. Okay, I still liked the colour, but I was more subtle with it now.

"It's not so bad." He sat down on the edge of the bed and bounced a couple of times. "All we really need is enough space." He grabbed my hands and pulled me to stand between his legs.

"I'm starting to think a bed is optional," I teased.

He responded with a boyish grin and, keeping hold of my hands, guided me down to the carpeted floor. He lay over me and pinned my hands above my head.

"As it happens, I don't care where I fuck you. Bed, carpet, shower, out on the front lawn for all the neighbours to see."

I smiled up at him. "It might be a bit cold out there for that."

"We'll put that on the list of things to do in summer," he said. "I bet we can give the whole neighbourhood quite the show." He lowered his mouth to mine, kissing me slowly and tracing all the way around my lips with the tip of his tongue.

I worked my legs out from under him and wrapped them around his waist, so his cock was neatly placed between my thighs. Even with our clothes between us, I could feel him getting harder.

He kissed my neck and gripped the top of my blouse. "Are you sure? I don't want to move too fast for you. If you want to get to know each other first, I'm okay with it."

Having him this close, and knowing Brock was listening, I was aroused as fuck. But not so aroused that I couldn't take a moment to think carefully and clearly.

He was right, this was going quickly, and we didn't have to rush into anything if we didn't want to. I knew if I said I wanted to stop, he'd honour that and stop immediately.

Did I want that? Was this a reaction to Mitch and Jagger keeping me at arm's length? My way of getting back at them? Was I turned on because I knew Brock would hear us fucking? I didn't want to use Kage for either of those reasons. I didn't want this to happen for the sake of it. If I was going to fuck him just to have someone to fuck, then we *should* stop.

But then, the more I thought about it, the more I realised that wasn't what this was. Kage was attractive; I enjoyed his company. I could see our relationship developing further. How far? I wasn't sure, but this wasn't just a fling for the heck of it. This was sex with someone I could come to care deeply for. I wanted to explore that, starting now.

"Don't stop," I said finally.

He pulled down the front of my blouse and a cup of my bra, before tracing circles around my nipple with his tongue.

"Delicious," he said. He gave the same treatment to the other nipple.

When he released my hands to pull my blouse off the rest of the way and unhook my bra, I let them wander over his hard body. Under his shirt and over firm muscles.

"I'll say," I agreed. I grabbed the back of his shirt and pulled it up so he could tug it off over his head. His body was as toned as any of the players on the team. He retired from playing hockey, but obviously still put in the work to stay in shape.

I rolled us over so I was on top of him, and undid the front of his jeans. Slowly, I worked down the zipper, and eased them open to free his erection.

"Is having a big cock a requirement for playing professional hockey?" I asked.

He chuckled. "No, some of us are just blessed."

He certainly was. His cock was long and thick, pulsing with blood and veins. A bead of pre-cum glistened on his tip. Until my tongue darted out and licked it off.

My eyes locked on his, I swirled my tongue around his tip before lowering my mouth onto his length.

He groaned. "Fuck yeah. That feels so good."

I smiled around my mouthful and went on sucking for a couple of minutes before he swivelled around and pulled my leg over him so my pussy was right in front of his mouth.

He caressed my clit and folds with his fingers, before licking all the way up and back down my seam.

I shivered at the sensations that went all the way

through my body at the lightest of his touch. The more he licked, the more I wanted. The more I needed.

He went on licking, driving me closer and closer to the edge. Right before I pitched over, he swivelled around again, rolled us over and pressed his cock deep inside my body. Slowly at first, until he was seated all the way to his balls.

"You feel incredible," he said, his eyes half closed as he savoured the feeling of us being joined so intimately. So perfectly.

"So do you," I said. He filled me so well, it was blowing my mind and making me even more aroused.

He raised his hips and thrust deeper into me. Carefully, deliberately, like we had all night.

He ran a hand from my throat, down my chest and between us to rub over my clit while he kept up his even strokes. In moments, he had me back on the edge, my body aching for more.

"You're so fucking beautiful," he said. "Let me see you come. Let me hear you. Remember, your stepfather is listening."

I didn't bother to correct him, remind him Brock wasn't my stepfather anymore. Kage's words seemed to be deliberate, wanting to provoke us both into reaching new heights of pleasure. Adding a level of taboo to the situation. I had no idea he was so naughty, but I liked it. For a while, I'd share that fantasy with him. The one where Brock was the last person who should be listening to us fuck.

He paused for a moment to draw my legs up, over his shoulder. When he thrust again, it was even deeper than before. He touched me all the way through, like our bodies might fuse together. His cock hit me inside with each stroke, like he knew exactly where to find my G spot and how to drive me absolutely wild.

"I'm going to come," I said loudly. Loud enough for Brock to hear. Hell, the neighbours probably heard, but I didn't give a shit right now.

"Come for me," Kage insisted. "Nice and loud."

I held onto him with my legs while I came so hard every nerve in my body felt it. A cry tore from my lips, so loud and raw, my throat was going to hurt later. I didn't give a shit about that either. All I knew was right here, right now and what his body was doing to mine.

And then what my body was doing to him, as my orgasm stole one from him. He let out a shout to match mine, as his body went still. He grunted and thrust a few more times, spilling himself into my body and milking his orgasm and mine for every single toe curling drop.

He panted for a few moments before easing my legs back down to the floor. "That was an amazing round one." He let me catch my breath before scooping me up in his arms and carrying me up to my bed.

"Now, we take our time getting to know each other." He lowered his mouth to mine and kissed me while he started a long, slow exploration of my entire body.

CHAPTER 11
BROCK

I've never been so hard in my fucking life, and that was before Eden brought her date home.

I ate a microwave dinner in front of the TV, while thinking about her and Kage Foster. I wasn't completely sure she'd bring him home, if I'm honest. She wanted to, I knew that. I was almost certain he'd agree to it. But, like everything in life, there's always the element of the unknown.

If that eventuated, I'd adjust. Plan B was almost as good as plan A. If he didn't fuck her, I'd fuck her myself. That would be no hardship for either of us.

Ideally, though, I wanted to draw out the anticipation of that moment. For her and for me. I'd waited so long for her my balls ached, but I wanted to savour the lead up for a while more. For years, I'd tortured myself with the idea of being with her. If it would happen.

That 'if' was now a firm, throbbing 'when.'

I finished my dinner, showered and went to bed. I lay awake, listening for the sound of the door opening and closing.

Smiled at the sound of two voices. Like the good slut she was, Eden was making no attempt to keep her voice down.

They entered her bedroom. Conveniently beside mine. I'd hear almost everything.

What I couldn't hear, I'd picture.

Starting with Eden lying naked, looking up at the head coach. From the sound of it, they were on the floor, even closer to the shared wall between our rooms. Perfect.

I lay on my bed in the dark, my hand curled around my already erect cock. Slowly, I worked my hand up and down my length, imagining it was Eden's mouth instead. Imagining her mouth on Kage's cock. Her lips sliding up and down, her tongue teasing him. It wouldn't be long until I felt that mouth for myself.

In the meantime, I listened carefully, breathlessly, as they changed positions.

I imagined I could hear her breathing, ragged, fast exhales and gasped inhales. In truth, I could make out breathy little moans, before she called out that she was coming.

I worked my cock harder, pre-cum making my hand slick. My balls grew heavier, heavier, the closer she came to coming.

"Come for me," I whispered.

In her room, Kage told her the same thing.

Like the perfect slut she was, she did as we told her to, screaming out to tell the world of her orgasm.

Hearing her like this was almost as good as hearing it from her lips when they were centimetres from my ear. Imagining Kage buried deep inside her, that was as arousing as me touching her pussy before she went on her date.

It was well past time she knew the truth, that she understood she belonged to me. I'd waited a long time to stake my claim on her. Now I had, I'd make her understand what that meant. I was going to have her in every way imaginable. She was going to take what I gave her and she was going to love every moment of it.

Hearing her come was compelling, but it was Kage's orgasm that pushed me into one of my own. His grunting as he spilled his cum into her body made mine squirt out to cover my hand, hot and slick.

Eden would take my cum, but the thought of her full of his made me smile. My smile widened as they moved to her bed and continued giving each other pleasure.

It was going to be a perfect night.

"Morning." I nodded to Kage over my cup of coffee. Eden, and her mother before her, always insisted I eat a proper breakfast. Ignoring them and only drinking coffee was a tradition around here now. Would that stop Eden from nagging me? Probably not. Would it make a difference? Nope. No one ever said I wasn't a stubborn bastard.

Kage nodded. "Morning. Enjoy the show?" Apparently he was as inclined to beat around the proverbial bush as I was.

If he was going to be blunt, he'd get that in return.

"Yep." I nodded again. "There's nothing quite like listening to that woman come." Kage too, but I'd keep that to myself for now.

"There really isn't," Kage agreed. "You good with sharing her?" He glanced back in the direction of the bathroom.

The shower was running. Picturing Eden naked while the hot water poured down her body made my dick twitch, ready again, even after a workout last night.

Later, I assured him.

"Yeah, you?" I nodded towards the mugs I'd put beside the electric kettle. "Help yourself."

He started to make himself a coffee. "I'm good with it. I wouldn't have minded if you joined us last night." He glanced over his shoulder at me, his expression measured.

"In time," I said. "She and I still have some things to work through."

"Her mother?" he guessed. "She's not on board with this?"

"She doesn't know," I said. "When she does, she's going to be pissed off." I saw no reason he shouldn't know the full story. If he was in, he was all in. When it came to Eden, she deserved nothing less. No half-assed bullshit. No lies or secrets. No nasty surprises when her mother appeared. She would, sooner or later. We'd be ready.

Paula was the one who cheated on me, but she always liked to place the blame for her actions on me. For marrying her when my heart was somewhere else.

I never admitted where, but I knew she always suspected there was someone else involved. Someone I couldn't have, so I settled for her. I cared about her, but that was never enough, not for either of us. We were never going to last, but I was grateful for the years I got to be involved in Eden's life in the meantime.

Watching her get older and grow comfortable in her own skin, grow ready for me. That was everything. Totally worth having to pretend I was in love.

"That's what Eden is worried about," Kage said carefully. "She doesn't want to hurt her mother."

I shrugged. "Paula left us. She didn't insist Eden go with her. Didn't even try. Wouldn't have mattered. Eden wasn't leaving Opal Springs. She wasn't leaving me. I wouldn't have allowed her to."

His eyebrows rose. "I didn't realise you had so much influence with her."

"I've known her for a long time. I know what to say to bring her around to my way of thinking." And if she tried to leave, I would have handcuffed her to my bed until she changed her mind. I might do that anyway. The cuffs were there, ready.

My cock was harder now.

"Right." He poured his coffee and set it on the counter, steam rising into the cool air. "So you gave her permission to go out with me last night?"

"In a manner of speaking," I said honestly.

I wanted to claim outright that I'd done exactly that, but I hadn't disagreed with her plans. If I had, things might have gotten heated. She might have ended up in those handcuffs, instead of on that date.

Now my balls were throbbing.

"And you've given her permission to go out with Mitch and Jagger?" Kage picked up his mug and blew across the top to cool it.

"Kinda," I said. "What are those two fucking around for? She was stomping around here like a sad panda for the last few days. Until yesterday."

Kage seemed amused at that analogy. "I put it down to youthful ignorance," he replied. "Once I stated my interest in her, they realised exactly where they stood."

"They didn't realise what they had until she was almost gone?" I guessed.

I worked my jaw back and forth in annoyance. If they weren't going to appreciate her the way she deserved to be appreciated, I'd kick their asses. And forbid them from seeing her.

"Something like that," Kage said. "But I think they

understand now. They both got territorial when I approached. They consider her theirs too."

I grunted. We'd see about that.

"What are these asshats like?" I met them and made my own quick judgement, but he knew them better than I did. Not that I trusted his judgement more than my own, but I was curious, and Kage seemed trustworthy. I wasn't trusting by nature, but he might be one of the better ones. Time would tell.

"Mitch is a good guy," Kage said slowly. "Jagger is too, but he's one of the grumpiest players I've ever met. And believe me, I've met a few. Played with a lot of them too. They usually have a chip on their shoulder the size of Sydney Harbour. "

Yeah, that was my assessment of both of them too. It seemed Kage and I were on the same page. I wondered if he liked to obey, or did he only bark out orders?

"Sounds like he needs to get over himself," I remarked. "If he's going to be a part of this, he better get his head out of his ass."

Kage grinned. "Those were my thoughts. But Eden and Mitch like him, and so do I. Between us, we'll work on him."

"You better, or he's out," I said bluntly. I wasn't having anyone involved with Eden who treated her like shit. Not when she had three other men who wouldn't.

"Would you be out if Eden had to choose between you and her mother?" Kage asked. "Are you prepared to put her in that *position?*"

It was obvious to me that he used that word on purpose, to get a reaction out of me.

I didn't so much as blink. I was used to dealing with worse than him at work.

"I wouldn't be putting her in that position," I said. "If there's any problem, it will come from her mother. She can accept the situation or not."

"You don't think she will?" Kage asked.

He didn't look convinced that the blame wouldn't be mine, at least in part. Honestly. It didn't matter much to me what he thought. Eden was mine. Paula could accept that, or not. If she chose to make it a problem, that was up to her. If I had to fight her for Eden, then so be it. I'd fight. Dirty if I had to.

"If she doesn't, we'll be here for Eden," I said. "If you're not down for that, then you can fuck off right now."

He held up his spare hand. "I'm down for it. Now I've had a taste of her, I don't want to walk away."

I noted my approval. "The woman is addictive." I was obsessed with her and I didn't want any help to get over that.

"I've noticed that," he said. "She seems to have you, me and my two players wrapped around her pretty little finger."

I looked at him through my brows. "She might have you wrapped around her pretty little finger, but she's wrapped around mine."

If I had my way, and I usually did, they'd all be

wrapped around mine. They'd fuck her when and how I told them to, and she take all of their cocks like the obedient slut she was.

"I'm starting to like you," Kage said. "I can appreciate a man who knows what he wants and doesn't pull any punches. It's refreshing."

"Get used to it," I said. "This is who I am. I'm not changing for anyone, not even Eden."

"I respect that," he said. "As head coach, I'm used to telling people what to do and having them listen."

"Are we going to have a problem?" I asked. "You're not going to expect me to do what you say, are you?"

"I have a feeling you only do what you want to do," he said. "But I might have fun watching."

I regarded him for a moment. "Yep, watching is good. Joining in is good."

He looked at me, searching, trying to decipher the exact meaning of my words. Apparently I was too hard to read, because he said, "How much joining in?"

I looked back at him. "Depends how much you like being on your knees."

His throat bobbed as he swallowed hard. "It's been a while."

I nodded and leaned over to pat his shoulder. "Take some time to get used to the idea. I'm going to give you and Eden a workout." When I was done with both of them, they'd be begging to obey me.

CHAPTER 12
EDEN

Brock watched from the front porch as Jagger pulled his car up to a stop in front of the house. He raised his beer to toast me, then turned his face back into the late afternoon sun. The night would be cold, but the front of the house was pleasant at this time of day. And if it wasn't, he'd sit there anyway, keeping an eye on me.

Neither he nor Kage told me what they talked about while I was in the shower the other morning, but Kage looked flustered when I stepped out to grab breakfast. Not necessarily flustered in a bad way, so I let it slide, in spite of my curiosity. That didn't stop me from speculating.

If something happened between them, they knew they had my full support. As long as I wasn't left out if they coupled up. Ditto with Mitch and Jagger.

I mean, I'd be happy for them, but it would sting for a while.

"You getting in or what?" Jagger called out from inside his black Ute.

Mitch punched him on the arm before he got out of the passenger seat and slid into the back seat, leaving me to sit beside Jagger. "Have some manners."

"Fuck off," Jagger snapped. "I have manners."

"Then use them," Mitch said before shutting the door behind him.

Jagger raised his hand and flipped him off, before greeting me with a nod. "You look hot."

"Thanks." I slipped into the seat and pulled the door shut. "Mitch said to dress casually." I'd chosen a low-cut crop top, with high-rise jeans and boots with heels. Chunky, they were almost high enough to make me as tall as the guys. Casual, with a hint of sass.

"I was going to say that," Mitch complained.

"Don't let me stop you," Jagger said. He peeled the Ute away from the curb and through the streets of Opal Springs.

"Hey Eden, you look hot," Mitch said.

I turned around in my seat to smile at him. "Thanks. You don't look so bad yourself."

Both guys wore jeans and dark button-down shirts. Casual, but they looked like models. Wherever we were going, I was going to get stared at by jealous women. And men.

Let them stare. I wasn't going to let it bother me. The guys were with me, not anyone else. On an actual date. A flutter of excitement passed through me. Would this change anything between us, or make us closer than ever? I hoped for the latter. I pushed away the sliver of doubt in the back of my mind that suggested getting to know each other better might ruin things between us. I knew the guys better than that. Deep down, we all knew there was more to us than being fuck buddies. I had to hold onto that and let time prove that right.

"Where are we going?" I asked.

"You'll see," Jagger said. His expression gave away nothing.

"Trust us, it'll be awesome," Mitch said. After a beat or two, and with unnecessary lightness, he added, "How was your night out with Kage?" He was clearly curious about more than our date.

"It was nice," I said. I told them about the restaurant and agreed they should go there sometime. They'd love the food as much as Kage and I had.

"Did you fuck him?" Jagger asked, apparently done with being patient. "Kage looked smug as hell the morning after."

"You didn't ask him?" I asked. I was surprised they hadn't outright confronted him. Jagger, in particular, didn't usually bother to hold back.

"We were busy with drills and he was busy with other stuff," Mitch said. "Besides, it was pretty obvious you did. Was it good?" He sounded slightly anxious. Was he worried Kage was better in bed than he and Jagger were?

"He was amazing," I said. "Just as amazing as you two."

Jagger grunted. "Doubt it. Mitch and I are next level, and we know what you like."

"Next time, you can watch and see for yourself," I said lightly, but with a hint of challenge.

Was it my imagination, or had the testosterone level in the car gotten thicker in the last minute or two? Were they actually insecure about their skills in bed? They didn't need to be. I'd lost track a long time ago exactly how many orgasms they'd given me each, much less between them.

"That sounds like a plan," Mitch said. "He's always welcome to join in with us. Right Jag?"

Jagger shrugged one shoulder. "I guess so. What about Brock? Did you sort things out with him?"

I pressed my lips together for a few moments. "Sort of. He... He definitely wants to get involved with me, but he wants to start by listening to me being fucked. He wanted me to bring Kage back home so he could hear us, and he wants to hear me with both of you as well."

"So your former stepfather listened to you fuck our head coach?" Mitch asked. He sounded awed. "That's hot." He wiped the back of his hand over his forehead, like he was dripping in sweat. He dropped his hand to his lap and grinned. "I'm happy to put on a performance, any time. Watching, listening, whatever."

"As long as they don't film it," Jagger said. "If that

shit gets out, the Ghouls' PR department will be pissed off. We're supposed to have squeaky clean images or some shit."

"Obviously they don't know Jagger very well," Mitch teased. "He's anything but squeaky clean."

I looked back at him. "What does that make you then?"

He grinned. "I'm the poster child for squeaky clean. I have the kind of face that lets me get away with pretty much everything. I always have."

With his blonde hair, blue eyes and dimples in his cheeks, I could totally see that. I bet kid-Mitch took full advantage of the fact. His parents and teachers never stood a chance.

"If they only knew what you're like behind closed doors," I teased. "Your image would go up in flames."

"Yeah, if they saw the way he sucked my cock, they wouldn't think he was so sweet and innocent," Jagger said.

My mind immediately went back to the last time I watched Jagger fuck Mitch's mouth. The memory alone was so hot I was ready to go up in flames. I loved watching them touch each other. I loved feeling them touch me. They held nothing back. Just like they did out on the ice.

"No, they'd be jealous instead," Mitch said lightly. "I have a talented mouth."

Both Jagger and I hummed our agreement. Mitch's

mouth on my pussy was one of my favourite things. Along with all the other things we did.

"This is it," Jagger said finally. He turned the car off the road, and onto a field at the edge of town. In the centre of the field stood a massive screen. A few metres back from that was a post with speakers dangling from it.

He stopped the car beside the post and killed the engine.

A food truck with 'Tanya's Tacos' down the side was parked a few metres away from us.

"You made a drive-in movie theatre?" I asked in amazement.

"Complete with tacos," Mitch said cheerfully. "Just for tonight and just for us."

"You guys." I shook my head.

Jagger wound down his window and reached out for the speaker, to pull it inside. "Tanya is only sticking around for a while, so let's get food before the movie starts."

When it came to tacos, I didn't need to be told twice. I hopped out of the car and headed over to the truck, the guys on either side of me.

"What will it be?" Tanya was around the same age as me. She played for the Opal Springs women's rugby union team. She had the build for it. Her shoulders were at least twice the size of mine. On the field, she was as tough as they got, but off the field she was one of the sweetest people I knew. Plus, because playing women's rugby didn't pay very well, she sold tacos for a living.

Anyone involved with tacos was a good person in my book.

"Why don't we get a selection and share?" Mitch suggested.

"I'm good with sharing," Jagger said, sliding me a look.

"That sounds perfect," I said.

"Coming right up," Tanya said easily. She turned to grab a cardboard box, and filled it with every kind of taco and burrito she sold. She also added some nachos, along with all the toppings we might want. She handed that box over, then a large cooler.

"Tacos aren't tacos without beer," Mitch said. "We weren't sure if you liked margaritas." A frown flitted briefly over his brow.

"Beer is fine," I said.

When I looked at the guys questioningly, Tanya said, "Everything was paid for in advance. Including this." She handed over another box, this one with the lid closed.

"That's for after dinner," Mitch said. "Don't open it."

I took the box and held it carefully. "Not even a peek?"

"No fucking peeking," Jagger insisted.

We headed back to his Ute as Tanya closed the side of the truck and headed away.

Jagger lowered the front seats, to stop them from

blocking our view. Mitch picked up his phone. He tapped the screen and the movie screen came to life.

"The latest superhero movie," he said with a grin.

All three of us slid into the back seat, me in the centre, between the two centres.

"Excellent," I said. I set the box aside at my feet and picked up a chicken taco before smothering it in sour cream and slices of avocado. Nobody made tacos better than Tanya.

I bit into mine and moaned at the delicious flavours that flooded through my mouth.

"If you keep making noises like that, we won't get through the movie," Mitch said.

Still chewing, I smiled at him. It wouldn't be the first time we'd missed the end of one. Sometimes, we even went back to watch what we hadn't the first time around.

"Such a brat," Jagger said, half under his breath.

I turned to look at him and snorted softly. I swallowed and said, "I learned from the best."

"Mitch," he stated.

"She meant you, dumbass," Mitch said. "Although, I've been called a brat before."

"If the helmet fits," Jagger said, "wear it with fucking pride."

"Oh, I do," Mitch said. He bit into his own taco and groaned. He said something unintelligible. Swallowed. Tried again. "This is good." He licked the side of his hand when the juices were running.

"The best," I agreed. I sat back to eat and watch the movie.

Every now and again, I snuck a glance at the gorgeous men to either side of me. Mitch looked entranced with the movie, but every so often he'd look over at Jagger and me.

Jagger was doing his best to look like he was interested in the movie, but his body language suggested he was more intent on me and Mitch. And eating as many tacos as he could fit into his stomach.

I wouldn't have thought we could get through that much food, but somehow, we managed. When the food was as delicious as this, we had to. It would have been a crime to waste it.

We washed the food down with plenty of beer, but not enough to get messy. Just enough to get a nice, happy buzz on top of the one I had from spending time with them on an actual date. One they'd clearly put a lot of thought and effort into. I never would have thought of doing this myself. Not in a million years.

"Are you having a nice time?" Mitch asked softly.

"I'm having a lovely time," I agreed. "How could I not? Amazing food, and amazing company. The movie isn't bad either."

"Do you want to see what's for dessert?" Mitch asked.

"Apart from me?" I asked with a half laugh.

"You're second dessert," Jagger said. He scooped up

the box from beside my feet and held it up for me to open the lid.

My eyes widened. "Ohhh, my favourite."

I was stuffed full of tacos, but I'd make room for chocolate cupcakes. Especially ones with sprinkles of chocolate on top of the icing.

"We know," Jagger said.

"You mean I know," Mitch said. "Jagger didn't have a clue."

Jagger shrugged. "Now I do. Are you going to take one?"

I picked up a cupcake and bit into it. It was so perfectly moist and sweet, I couldn't help half closing my eyes and groaning. I was starting to feel very spoilt and I didn't mind for a moment.

CHAPTER 13
EDEN

Somehow, we managed to get to the end of the movie without fucking.

We finished the cupcakes and beer—an interesting taste combination—and the guys sat with one hand in my lap. I sat with each of mine in theirs. Their cocks were erect and straining, and my pussy was wet, but we restrained ourselves. Not because we didn't want to interrupt the movie, but I suspected we all had the same thing on our minds.

The fact this was an actual date, and Brock listening to us when we moved onto our second dessert.

The way he touched me the other night before Kage picked me up lingered in my thoughts. That and the promise I'd made. I wanted to do what he'd told me to do. I wanted to obey when he said to bring them home for him to enjoy. The idea gave me more flutters of excitement, and made me so aroused, I might come with a glance from the right angle. I couldn't remember being more aroused in my life.

Admittedly, I was a little tempted to find out what Brock would do if I didn't bring the guys home for him. I had a feeling whatever it was, I'd like it. For now though, I wanted to enjoy both guys, and know my mother's former husband was right there on the other side of the wall. Listening as they fucked his former stepdaughter. Imagining himself doing those things to me.

I wanted him to. Now I'd given in to that first bit of temptation, I wanted more of it. I didn't care if he'd fucked my mother with his cock, I wanted to feel him sliding it into my pussy. I wanted him to pound into me before spilling himself into my body. I wanted to scream out his name when he made me come.

I'd seen the handcuffs on his bed and I wanted him to use them on me.

"What are you thinking?" Mitch whispered. "Are they dirty thoughts?"

I swallowed and nodded.

"Tell us," Jagger insisted. His voice was just as low, but more demanding.

"I was thinking about Brock restraining me on his bed," I whispered. "I was thinking how it would feel to have him on top of me. Inside me."

"What would he do to you?" Jagger asked. "What do you want him to do? Tell us what you picture in your head."

"I'm picturing myself lying on top of the covers, my hands above my head," I whispered. "In handcuffs. I'm picturing him with something sharp. A knife or a pair of scissors. He's cutting the clothes off my body. Snip by snip until I'm naked." I mimed a pair of scissors with my fingers.

"He's tossing the scraps of fabric aside. He's looking at me while he takes off his clothes. His cock is big and hard. Leaking."

"What do you want him to do with that cock?" Mitch asked.

"I want to spread my legs and let him ram it inside me," I said. I was so turned on, I might come if one of them blew on my clit.

"Picture him climbing on top of you," Jagger said. "You're spreading your legs to take him in. All of him, all the way to his balls."

I groaned. I swallowed hard to keep from touching myself.

"He's so big. I'm so full. He's thrusting inside me, moving slowly. He keeps looking at me, watching me while he's fucking me. He's calling me his slut and telling me to take all of him."

Everything was so clear in my mind, as though he was right there, his weight pressing down on me.

"You're our slut," Jagger said. "His and Kage's and ours. You're going to take all of our cocks, because that's what you're made for."

I moaned. "Please," I whispered. "I need to be fucked."

Mitch echoed my moan. "Fucking hell, I'm so hard."

"Then we need to get Eden home," Jagger said. "Both of you stay here in the back. Don't touch each other and don't touch yourselves."

Mitch grunted with annoyance, but nodded and placed his fists on his thighs to either side of his visible erection. "Drive fast or I'm going to lose my load in my jeans."

Jagger smirked. "Think unsexy thoughts. Think about losing the next five games in a row."

"That's not unsexy, that's a horror story," Mitch complained.

"Sorry, not sorry." Jagger pushed out of the car and hurried to the driver's seat. He put it back up and jumped in.

I didn't miss his wince as he landed on the seat. He adjusted his pants before he started the engine and headed home.

We barely got through the door before we were tearing at each other's clothes.

The house was in darkness. I presumed Brock was in bed, waiting once again for me to be fucked in mine. Part of me wanted to slip into his room and slide myself down his cock. But I had Jagger and Mitch to satisfy, and to satisfy me.

Plus, Brock told me he wanted to wait until he was ready to have me.

Somehow, we made it into my room and onto my bed. Mitch lay beside me and captured my mouth with his, while Jagger knelt between my knees and slammed his cock all the way into me, right to his balls.

I cried out in surprise and pleasure at the suddenness of his thrust.

"You're so fucking wet," he groaned. "So fucking good." He locked his eyes on mine. "Tell us what you are."

I was practically panting when I replied, "Your slut. I'm your slut!"

I pictured Brock's expression when he heard me cry those words out. Pictured his hand curling around his length.

"Jagger," I panted. "Fuck me as hard as you can. I want your cock, all of it. Fuck me like you hate me."

That was exactly what he did. He pulled all the way out and slammed back in with a fierce grunt. He pulled back out, rolled me over and pulled me up on to all fours. He grabbed hold of a fistful of hair and held me while he rammed back into me.

Over and over he slammed and slammed, while I cried out the combination of pleasure and pain. This was exactly what I needed tonight.

Mitch knelt beside me, turned my face toward him

and shoved his cock between my lips. "Our slut is going to take my cock too."

I opened my mouth and he pushed himself in until the head of his cock tapped my throat. I gagged, but I didn't pull away. Couldn't anyway, with Jagger holding me in place by my hair.

All the while, I pictured Brock, sliding his hand up and down his cock. A new image sprang into my mind. Kage lying beside him, doing the same to his own erection. Turning to Brock and working his at the same time. Brock leaning back against the headboard, eyes half-closed.

Mitch reached under me to roll my nipple between his thumb and forefinger, then pinched it.

I cried out with pleasure around my mouthful, but didn't stop sucking and teasing him with my tongue.

"You like that." He slid his hand from my breast, over my stomach and between my legs. He ran his fingers over my pussy, avoiding my clit until I looked at him, silently begging him to touch me there.

Eventually, he circled my clit with his fingertips. He barely touched, but it was enough to make me come, shuddering and screaming around his cock.

"Make her come again," Jagger said. He didn't slow his ceaseless thrusting, while his hand tightened in my hair. He held absolutely nothing back. Every centimetre, every pound, he put everything into each one. His cock hit me all the way through, filling me tight and hard.

"You heard the man," Mitch said. "He wants our slut

to come again. You're going to do what he says, aren't you?" He worked me with his fingers while fucking my mouth as hard as Jagger was fucking my pussy.

I managed a slight nod and sound of agreement in the back of my throat. I never thought I'd enjoy being called something like that, but when they did it, I wanted more of it. I wanted to be their slut. I wanted them to use me in every way possible. I wanted them to fuck me like they owned me. I'd take every bit, every drop.

More than that, I wanted them to fuck me like they hated me and wanted to take all of their anger out on me. Before, when we'd fucked, they'd both held back. We all had. I didn't want that anymore. I wanted us all to let go.

I closed my eyes and focused on sucking Mitch, working him with my mouth as hard as I could. I move my hips in rhythm with Jagger, grinding myself onto Mitch's hand. The rest of the world disappeared and all that was left was our bodies moving in sync, pants and groans, grunts and sweat.

I was so aroused, I was quick to come for a second time and then a third. On the last orgasm, Jagger and Mitch both came, straining and thrusting before they both went still, spilling their load into my pussy and down my throat.

Gasping, I pulled myself off Mitch's cock, but held his release in my mouth. I waited until Jagger slid out of me before I turned around and pressed my lips to his. I pushed my tongue between them, insisting he opened his mouth before I squirted Mitch's cum inside.

Jagger blinked a couple of times in surprise before swallowing it down and licking his lips. "Tasty."

"That was fucking hot," Mitch said. He flopped down onto the bed, his skin shining with perspiration.

I lowered myself down more carefully. My pussy hurt after the pounding Jagger gave me, but it was absolutely perfect. Pleasure and pain. And something more. Somehow, it felt intimate in a way sex with them hadn't felt before. I'd never felt so connected to both of them.

The voice in the back of my mind still held on to a whisper of doubt. Did they feel the same way?

CHAPTER 14
EDEN

For the first time since we met, I woke up with a hot hockey player on either side of me. Neither of them hurried to get dressed and leave the night before. Neither had bolted for the door the moment they came.

Instead, Mitch fucked me with his mouth, while Jagger fucked him from behind, then we all fell asleep. I woke up feeling sore, but rested. Relaxed in a way I'd never felt before.

Mitch snored softly, but Jagger was already awake. He watched me with those dark eyes, like a cat might watch a bird.

I rolled over to face him. "Morning."

He grunted in response. "Hey." He turned his face and yawned into the pillow, before stretching, his muscles rippling.

"Did you sleep well?" I asked.

"Like a rock." He yawned again, this time covering his mouth with his fist. He glanced at his watch.

For a moment I expected him to jump up and make a dash for the door. Instead, he nestled down deeper into the blankets and made no move to leave.

"I should probably have a shower," I said. I didn't have to open my shop for another couple of hours, but at some point I'd need to get up and head out. So would they; they had a game tonight. I didn't want to get them in trouble with Kage. Well, not professionally.

"We should get going," Jagger said reluctantly. "After I wash your back."

"That's going to lead to more than washing my back," I said with a sleepy smile.

"Yep." He pushed the covers off himself and grabbed my wrists to pull me over to the edge of the bed. Once there, he lowered his shoulder and scooped me up to drape me over, so my head was dangling over his back.

I let out a squeal of surprise, which woke Mitch.

"Now there's a view to wake up to," he said. From where he lay, he would have seen my ass and legs and not much more.

"You're welcome," Jagger deadpanned. He carried me into the bathroom that was connected to my bedroom and turned the water on in the shower. He didn't lower me down inside until the spray was nice and warm.

"You're a gentleman after all," I teased.

"Bullshit," he said lightly. His expression completely

mild, he gripped my shoulders and moved me out from under the water so he could step under it himself.

"Hey!" I protested. I shoved my shoulder into his bicep to push him out of the way. I was too small to move him, but he pretended to stagger out from under the water.

He shook his head, sending droplets of water flying.

"*Now* you won't share?" he asked.

"No one asked me how I felt about sharing," I said. Eyes on his, I started to wash my hair, standing firmly in the centre of the water.

"If you're going to be a brat, I'm going to have to punish you," he said.

"Are you threatening her with a good time?" Mitch stepped into the shower with us, his cock already half erect.

"No, I'm stating a fact," Jagger said over his shoulder. He stepped around behind me, blocking off the water for a moment before he grabbed my hair and pulled my head back so he could rinse off the shampoo.

"Is this punishment?" I asked.

"It will be if you don't keep your mouth shut," Jagger growled. "You'll get shampoo in there."

He had a point. I closed my mouth and eyes and let him work his hands through my hair. At the same time, Mitch started to wash the front of my body with body wash.

I cracked open half an eye, smiled at him, then curled my hand around his cock.

"If this is punishment, it needs to happen more often." Mitch thrust himself into my hand, his wet length sliding in and out of my fingers.

"This is just the start," Jagger said. He finished rinsing my hair and placed one hand on my shoulder. The other tangled in my hair, he pushed me to my knees in front of him. Holding me firmly, he guided my mouth onto his cock.

I parted my lips, letting him slide inside, all the way to the back of my throat. He stopped there, still for a few moments before sliding all the way back out and all the way back in.

"Fucking your mouth is one of my favourite hobbies." He thrust a few more times before sliding out of me and turning my face to Mitch's cock. "Watching him fuck your mouth is another one of them."

My head bobbed as I vigorously sucked. I ran a hand up Mitch's thigh, between his legs and over his balls. I did the same with my other hand on Jagger's balls.

Jagger groaned and moved me back to his cock. "Take me in deeper."

I opened my mouth as wide as it could possibly go, taking in as much of him as I could. With every stroke, he tapped the back of my throat. I gagged, but went on sucking and licking.

"Just like that," he said breathlessly.

I knew from the way he sounded and moved that he

was on the verge of coming. Right before he did, he moved me back to Mitch's cock.

"I like it when you're generous," Mitch told him.

"I'm always generous," Jagger growled. "Especially when it comes to Eden. She deserves to have her mouth, pussy and ass shared with all of us and all of our cocks. She likes it when we use all of her holes, don't you, Eden?"

I glanced up at him and let my eyes smile, while I went on working Mitch as hard as I could. At the same time, I didn't lessen the pressure on Jagger's balls. If he wanted me to stop, he'd say so.

"Of course she does." Mitch moved his hips back and forth, thrusting between my lips as though he was in no hurry at all. As if he could have done it all day. He probably could. Neither of them were prone to rushing, not usually. Only when we hadn't seen each other for a few days.

"That's why she has three holes." Mitch smiled. "All the better to take three cocks at a time, and one in her hand."

"That's why you have two," Jagger told him. "I want to see you with Kage when all three of us are together. I'll fuck your ass and he can fuck your mouth."

Mitch groaned and leaned over to kiss Jagger on the mouth. "I want that too," he said against the other centre's lips.

I moved my hand from Mitch's balls, down between my legs. Picturing all three of them together made me need to touch myself. Where would Brock factor into this? Maybe he and I would be to the side of them, him buried deep in my pussy while the three guys fucked each other.

His hand gripping my head tightly, Jagger pulled me back onto his own cock right before he came, squirting warm cum into my mouth.

"Don't swallow yet." He moved me back to Mitch's cock, guiding me back onto him, and moving me while Mitch thrust. "Come inside her mouth."

Mitch let out a series of ragged gasps before he too came, adding his cum to the mouthful I was already holding.

I pulled my lips off him and breathed through my nose, forcing myself not to swallow. I swished their combined cum around in my mouth as I rose to my feet with Mitch's help. I pressed my mouth to his, and pushed the cum between his lips.

It was his turn to swish the mouthful appreciatively. He nodded his approval before kissing Jagger and letting the cum dribble into his mouth.

Jagger grabbed the back of my head and pressed his lips to mine, passing the mouthful back to me. "Now you can swallow."

While he held me, I locked eyes on him and swallowed every delicious drop.

"Mitch, get on your knees and make her come," he ordered.

"Yes, Coach," Mitch said smartly. He knelt down in

front of me and parted my legs, before diving in with his mouth and tongue.

Jagger held me firmly in place, one hand hooked under my knee to keep my legs apart for Mitch.

Mitch pressed a couple of fingers into me and hooked them around to stroke my G spot while his tongue worked my clit.

"You're enjoying that, aren't you?" Jagger asked.

"Very much," I whispered.

"Louder," he said. "We want Brock to hear."

"Very much," I said, loud enough for the sound to pass through the walls.

"What are you going to do for us?" Jagger asked.

"I'm going to come," I said. "I'm going to come for you, Mitch and Brock." Brock's name came out as a moan.

"Yes, you are," Jagger said. "Nice and loud. Tell Opal Springs just how much of a slut you are for us."

I groaned, letting him support most of my weight, while I put everything into grinding against Mitch's mouth, all of my concentration going into doing what he told me to do.

When I came, it was hard, deep and loud. My scream of pleasure echoed through the bathroom, competing with the rush of blood through my ears and pleasure through my entire body. I came so fucking hard I could have literally shattered into a million pieces without knowing it, before coming back together.

When I finally came back down from my high, I was

boneless. If it wasn't for Jagger holding me up, I would have flopped down to the tiles and disappeared down the drain in a puddle. He held me until I was able to hold myself.

"That's how you do it," he told me. "It's time to get out of here. Let's get dry."

I let him help me out of the shower and wrapped myself in a towel. I could definitely get used to this.

CHAPTER 15
KAGE

"Looks like you had a good time last night." I stopped beside Mitch and Jagger as they were getting ready for tonight's game. They had matching satisfied, smug expressions on their faces. The one that comes with getting laid.

Mitch adjusted his padding and grinned. "The best time. Right, Jag?"

"Yep," Jagger said, his usual bare bones answer.

Mitch elbowed him. "Don't pretend you didn't."

"I'm not pretending anything," Jagger protested. He elbowed Mitch back. "What do you want, a blow by blow description of the whole night? And this morning?" He glared at Mitch, but there was a hint of playful mischief in his eyes that was new.

"I'll take that as a yes," I said, with an approving nod. "Good, I'm glad you're enjoying our girl. I was thinking we should surprise her by doing something together. All four of us." Or five, if Brock was included. Thinking about him made my cock throb, but I wasn't sure where he fit into all of this yet.

"Sooner or later, she's going to want a group date. I want to get in before it even occurs to her. Between us, I'm sure we can come up with something that'll impress her."

Was I going too fast with this? Potentially, but I wanted to do this for her. To show her how I felt about her. I could easily fall head over heels for Eden Wright. Where did that leave Brock? Did he want a relationship with any of us, or did he want to be the conductor of our little orchestra? He made it clear he wanted to fuck me, but how much further would it go? That was a question for later.

"This isn't an episode of *The Bachelor*," Jagger said derisively. "Group date?"

"How do you know they have group dates on that show?" Mitch looked at Jagger sideways, teasing curiosity on his face. He was too cute for his own good sometimes, but he kept Jagger on his toes.

Jagger rolled his eyes at the other centre. "Because I've seen you watch it, dumbass."

"Because he's watched it with me," Mitch whispered loudly.

Jagger's jaw moved like he was trying to protest. Finally, he said, "Only when there's nothing else on.

And I'm not watching it, I'm reading a book or on my phone. It's just on in the background."

"You were as invested in the relationship between Ashley and Brandon as I was," Mitch argued.

"I fucking was not," Jagger said. "But Brandon should have chosen Ashley, not Hannah. It doesn't matter anyway, he broke up with Hannah already."

"And you know that how?" I teased.

He turned his glare on me. "Mitch went on about it. He's obsessed with that crap."

Mitch rubbed his chin. "I don't remember mentioning that." He patted Jagger on the bicep. "It's okay to admit you looked it up."

Before Jagger could respond, I said, "It's time to get out there on the ice. Give them hell."

"We always do," Jagger said with a grunt. He grabbed up his stick and stomped towards the door.

From here, the sound of the crowd was audible, as was the music playing out in the rink. The excitement was electric. And contagious. It helped to tamp down my nerves somewhat.

Even after working with the team for two years, I was still nervous for them. We'd worked so hard to move the team to a professional level. Now they had to prove they deserved that, over and over. None of them wanted to go back to amateur status. Every so often, the conversation arose, and everyone was in agreement. They were going to fight to keep their spot in the AIHL, no matter what it took.

And me, I was happy to kick their asses into gear when they needed it. The same way I'd had my ass kicked when I was playing. Did I miss the rush of being out there, stick in hand, taking on the highly skilled teams in the NHL? Sometimes. But we'd made something special here and I had no regrets about making the move.

"For what it's worth, I think that's a good idea," Mitch said before grabbing his stick. "The group date thing. I think she'll like it." He shot me a grin before following Jagger out to warm up.

At the beginning of the fourth period, the Dusk Bay Demons were leading five to four. The Ghouls were quick and aggressive, but the opposition was faster, hungrier.

Under their new owners, the Demons were virtually unstoppable. If we weren't careful, they'd dominate from the moment the season started and take out the whole thing.

I was determined not to let that happen. We weren't going down without a fight.

The puck dropped.

Jagger snapped out his stick, gaining possession of the biscuit and slamming it past Coast Riggs. It slid across the ice, past the Demons' winger, and straight to Easton, who'd skated around to intercept.

Easton took a shot at goal, but Phoenix, the Demons' goalie, stopped the puck at the last second.

Jagger and Mitch switched out, and the Demons had possession of the puck. They wove through our guys, shoving them out of the way and slamming them against the boards.

The Ghouls fought back, a couple of them letting their frustration get the better of them.

I shouted at them to chill out before changing out a couple of the players when the Demons missed a shot at goal.

The puck was back in our possession, with Jagger switching again with Mitch. His face a mask of determined concentration, he drove the puck deep into opposition territory. Again, Easton was there to intercept. He slammed it back to Jagger, who swept it straight into the goal, past Phoenix's glove.

"And we have a tie!" The announcer declared over the loudspeaker. "We might just go into overtime." She sounded delighted at the prospect. Why wouldn't she? Everyone liked a close fought, nail biting game. Although, I personally didn't mind a shut out either.

We might just, I silently agreed. Unless we could close it out now. Forcing the game to a tie with a team as strong as the Demons, gave the players confidence. It might just be enough to see them through until the end of the period.

Another face-off, this time with Mitch back on the

ice. The Demons' centre was quicker this time, slapping the puck away the second it touched the ice.

They drove it hard towards our goal, but the Ghouls weren't letting them anywhere near it. They shoved back and blocked every shot, until I thought gloves might come off.

While fighting was discouraged in the league, it happened, like it did with the NHL. During some games, it felt like blood flowed more freely than water at the break between periods.

I glanced at the time. The clock was counting down the seconds till the end of the period. Unless something happened in the next couple of heartbeats, overtime was inevitable.

Five.

Four.

Three.

Two.

One.

The buzzer finally sounded, giving us a break. Overtime wouldn't stop until one team or the other scored. We need to be ready.

"You guys are kicking butt out there," I said. "You've got this. The Demons are on the run now. All we need to do is finish them off."

I caught the eye of Aidan Draeger, the Demons' head coach. He was a difficult man at the best of times, but he gave me a respectful nod before turning back to talk to his own team. He'd supported the Ghouls, voting for them to become a professional team, when the rest of the committee was still unsure. That didn't mean I wouldn't push my guys to beat his. Anything else would be an insult to all of us. They wouldn't hold back and neither would we.

"We've got this, Coach," Mitch said, cheerful and loud. "Right team?"

"Shit, yeah, we do," Cruz agreed. "It's time to hand those Demons their asses on a silver platter. This is our season to take out the cup."

The guys all shouted their agreement with fierce determination. Being one of the newer teams in the AIHL they were always under a microscope. There were those still convinced the league made a mistake in choosing us, but we'd prove them wrong.

I glanced back at Aidan. He was nodding at something one of the Demons' owners said. I didn't know much about the Brantley twins, but they seemed to care about their team more than the previous owner. For that, I'd give them all the credit they deserved.

Before them, and before Aidan, the Demons were the biggest losers in the league. Now, they were difficult to beat. As a team, they were cohesive and united. The rest of us could learn something from watching them interact on and off the ice. They had a bond I'd never seen before with any team. Something I worked towards with mine.

Hashtag team goals.

Coming second to them in the play-offs would suck,

but it wouldn't be the end of the world. Of course, beating them would be better.

I nodded to my team. "Okay, time to get out there and get this done. Don't let them touch the puck and we can finish this off in a minute or two."

"On it, Coach." Mitch gave me a salute before all the guys put their water bottles aside and took their positions, either on the ice, or waiting to celebrate.

"That sucked hairy donkey balls." Mitch was still smiling, but his shoulders were slightly slumped. He tossed his stick roughly in the direction of his locker and flopped down onto the seat in front of it.

Some of the guys headed off to burn off excess lactic acid, but Jagger sat beside Mitch and gripped his shoulder. He shook him a couple of times before slapping his bicep.

"We'll get them next time," Jagger said.

"Exactly," I agreed. "You guys put up a good fight. There's no reason why we can't win the next game against them." They'd come painfully close to doing just that tonight.

They'd lost possession of the puck right before making a shot at goal and never got it back. With an assist from the Demons' centre, their winger made the deciding goal.

The moment after that happened, I spotted Eden in

the team box. She'd been cheering us on the entire game, Marley and Cat beside her. She gave me a wave and even blew me a kiss. I responded with a small wave of my own, and a silent promise to see her soon, before turning my attention back to the team.

"I need a shower." Mitch started to pull off his skates and shed his clothes.

I watched for a few moments before forcing myself to look away. That was another thing we needed to work out. What might my relationship with them be like? I didn't know, but I knew having a boner for any member of the team, right here in the locker room, was probably not the most professional look for the head coach. Especially not with the rest of the team present.

Totally naked, Mitch stepped past me. On the way, he stopped and whispered in my ear, "I don't mind you looking." Grinning, he moved past and headed to the showers.

Apparently his usual good mood was back, in full force. Nothing ever kept him down for very long. He couldn't have been more different to Jagger. They were night and day in looks and personality. In their case, opposites definitely attracted. Not just attracted, but gelled together like a tight unit. They balanced each other, on and off the ice.

"Okay," I said slowly. I caught a glimpse of his bare ass before he disappeared into a shower cubicle. He didn't even close the door behind him, but the partition blocked him from view. The man was definitely not shy about his body. Neither was I; I was just trying to keep things cool and do my job without being too distracted. So much for not getting hard.

I shook my head and stepped out of the locker room. I had work to do before I could catch up with Eden and the others.

And planning to do for our group date.

CHAPTER 16
EDEN

All the guys would tell me was to pack an overnight bag with an outfit for a night out, and something for the next day.

Kage was very careful to say, "Don't bring any pyjamas. You won't be wearing any."

He was right on time to pick me up and drive me to the airport.

"Am I being abducted?" I asked.

He glanced over at me and grinned. "Yes. Yes, you are. By a whole hockey team."

"Sounds like a handful," I said, keeping my expression bland.

He chuckled. "They would be, but you only have to worry about two of them and one of me. Are you sure Brock is okay with this?"

"Sort of. He's working for the next three nights. His

exact words were, 'the next time the three of them are with you, I'll be taking part too.'"

"Shame he's missing out then," Kage said, his voice low.

This was the perfect opportunity to ask, "What did he say to you when you were alone in our place?"

Kage stiffened slightly. He focused on driving through the car park and into an empty spot. "It might be too fast."

"What might be?" He had me intrigued now.

Kage turned off the engine and twisted around to face me. "He told me he was going to make me suck his cock the next time we were together."

My mouth formed an O. My pussy formed a puddle.

"And how do you feel about that?" I didn't know if he was into other men or not. I was equally uncertain if Brock would give him a choice.

"I think I'd like to get to know him before he fucks my mouth," Kage said. He slid the keys out of the ignition and tucked them into his pocket.

Now I understood what he meant by being too fast. He and I had moved quickly enough. Him immediately moving on to giving Brock a blowjob would give us both whiplash.

"Then I'm happy to help you do that, if that's what you want," I offered. "Get to know him, I mean."

"Is that what you want?" Kage asked. "How would you feel about him and I fucking each other?"

"The same way I feel about Mitch and Jagger fucking each other," I said honestly. "If that's what they want to do, then I fully support it. And if you and Brock want to fuck each other, then I support that too." After a moment I added, "And any combination in between."

"It wouldn't be *instead* of being with you," Kage said quickly. "This might sound… I don't know." He glanced down in the direction of the handbrake.

"I see the relationships your friends have with their boyfriends. Their families. I want that too." He looked back up. "I want the kind of family where everyone cares about everyone else. Where everyone wants everyone else to be the best version of themselves. Where everyone wants to make everyone else feel good. I don't know if that's asking too much." His Canadian accent was stronger when he spoke like this. Hotter. I could listen to him talk all day.

I placed my fingers lightly on his stubbled cheek. "That's not asking too much at all. I want that too. Love, laughter, sex, all of it. With no one feeling like they need to hold back for any reason. Especially because they might be worried I'd be upset about it. If you want to suck Brock's cock, then I want that for you. If you want to suck Mitch and Jagger's, then I want that too. As long as I get my share of orgasms."

"I'll personally make sure of it," he said. He seemed relieved at my response. "I've had people turn away from me because of my sexual preference. But it's who I am, you know? I've always liked women and men. I can't change that. I don't want to. Other people though… Sometimes they don't get it."

I leaned over and pressed my forehead to his. "I totally get it. I wouldn't want to change you any more than I'd want to change Brock, Jagger or Mitch. I want to help you to explore what you want to explore and be comfortable with your sexuality and in your own skin. That's what family is for. To be there for you, no matter what."

"I could fall in love with you," he whispered. "I'm already halfway there."

"I could fall in love with you too," I said. "All of you."

In the back of my mind, was the niggling doubt about what my mother might say. Not just about Brock, but also about the difference in age between me and Kage, and whether it was possible to have a relationship like the one between Mitch and Jagger, and have one with me at the same time. She'd probably tell me to find a guy who only wanted me. That would only ever care about me and never glance at anyone else. Someone like her present partner. Someone not like Brock.

Part of me wondered if she might be right to say those things. What if Mitch and Jagger fell more deeply in love with each other than they did with me? What if Kage and Brock fell head over heels for each other, and I was left out in the cold? Hell, what if Mitch and Kage decided to dance off into the sunset together?

There were so many complications and so many variables, my head hurt to think about it. Should I ask Kage to turn the car around and take me home? Possibly, but I wasn't going to. I was here now and I wanted to see this all the way through, no matter the consequences.

"We should go before the plane leaves without us," Kage said reluctantly.

"Would they dare to leave without you?" I breathed in the scent of him, soap, coffee and a hint of nerves.

"Probably, yes," he said. "The boys would have a good laugh about it."

"Well, we won't give them the opportunity." I reluctantly pulled away and kissed his mouth before I followed him out of the car.

The plane was loud, but the trip to the Gold Coast was short. I remembered the last time I was here, with Marley. She was trying to get over her guys at the time, so I'd brought her here to give her some space. The time away was just what we both needed.

Now, I was here with three of my guys, who won their game against the local team before changing and whisking me away in, of all things, a stretch limousine.

"Where are you taking me?" I asked.

"You'll see," Kage said, his hand resting lightly on one of my knees.

Mitch's hand was resting on the other, while Jagger sat on the other side of him.

"Did I mention I don't like surprises?" I asked.

"I already told you, we're abducting you," Kage said with a boyish grin.

"Yes, but you didn't tell me *where* you were abducting me to," I pointed out.

"We're almost there," Mitch assured me. "Just another couple of minutes."

I pouted playfully, but looked out the window and watched the city turn into the suburbs, the late hour settling into a long night.

A few minutes later, the limousine turned off the main road and headed into the darkness. The headlights illuminated what looked like little more than a track.

"If I was going to abduct someone, I'd bring them somewhere like this," I said. "It looks perfect for a shallow grave."

Jagger snorted. "We didn't bring you here to kill you. Besides, we would have to kill the driver too. She's already seen too much."

"It seems like you've given this some thought," I teased.

He responded with the faintest hint of a smile before turning his face back toward the window.

"We won't let Jagger kill you," Mitch assured me. "He'd have to get past Kage and me, and that won't happen."

"I could get past both of you if I wanted to," Jagger said without looking back around.

"Keep telling yourself that," Mitch teased.

The limousine rolled to a halt, gravel crunching under the tyres.

"We're here," Kage said. He opened the door and stepped out before offering me his hand.

I took it and followed him out, leaving Mitch and Jagger to scramble out after me.

Jagger closed the door behind him and the limousine drove just out of sight. The driver turned off the headlights, leaving us in darkness except for the glow of the moon on the ocean not twenty metres from where we stood. The beach was totally deserted except for us. Well, us and about a million candles that flickered around a blanket spread out on the sand.

"When we abduct someone, we do it in style," Mitch said.

"So I see," I said, drinking in the sight. In the centre of the blanket was a cooler filled with ice, bottles of beer and one of champagne. Beside that was a plate with a cover over it.

The guys led me over to sit on the blanket.

"I asked Marley what your favourite food was," Kage said.

"She said tacos," Mitch said.

I'd already been treated to tacos at the stadium while the guys played. They weren't as good as Tanya's, but they were nice enough.

"We went with the second choice." Jagger picked up the plate and pulled off the cover to reveal chocolate covered strawberries.

"Marley said chocolate, but we wanted something a bit more romantic," Kage said. He picked up a strawberry and held it to my lips.

I opened my mouth and bit down on the luscious, sweet treat. I closed my eyes and groaned. "So good." I chewed and swallowed before he offered me the rest of it. "You guys organised this just for me?"

"Kage and Mitch decided you'd want a group date," Jagger said. "They did that part. I did this." He picked up a wide, flat box from behind the cooler and opened it. Inside was a palette of paint and a couple of small brushes.

"I didn't know you were an artist," I said.

He picked up a brush. "Only with the right canvas." He dipped the brush into the blue paint and raised it to my chest. "You might want to take your top off, this is going to get messy."

The night air here was warm, so I didn't hesitate to pull off my top and place it beside the cooler. I sat still in just a skirt, panties and my black lace bra.

Biting his lip with concentration, Jagger started to paint small lines and swirls on the skin of my chest. He sat back to admire his work before dipping the brush in the yellow and adding that to what he'd already done. Then a touch of pink, and a little green. He nodded to

Mitch, who unhooked my bra and slid it down my arms.

"Better," Jagger said. He painted a circle around one nipple, then the other. Leaning in, he seemed to be writing something on my left breast.

I glanced down to see the words, 'property of Jagger Sanderson.'

"You should get that tattooed, so it's permanent," Jagger said. "Lie down."

I did what he said and watched the candlelight flicker on his face as he painted swirls around my belly.

"You're the perfect canvas," he whispered.

"She looks incredible like this," Mitch said. He undid my skirt and slid it down my legs before placing it with my top.

"Better like that," Kage said. He was sitting back on his heels, watching carefully, his pants tenting more prominently by the moment.

"Does this paint wash off?" I asked.

"It's better than that," Jagger said as he dabbed spots on my thighs. "It's edible, so we get to lick it off."

CHAPTER 17
EDEN

"I volunteer as tribute," Mitch said. He knelt down beside my stomach and leaned over me to lightly lick at the paint with the tip of his tongue. "Mmm, strawberry and Eden flavoured. That's officially my favourite flavour. Right up there with Eden's pussy and the taste of cum."

"You have my curiosity." Kage leaned to lick yellow body paint off the side of my breast. "Pineapple and Eden. You taste better than a cocktail."

"That's a high endorsement," I said with a smile.

"Just stating a fact." He licked more of the paint off my breast before sucking it off my nipple.

"The blue tastes like blueberries," Mitch said. "Jagger, I've decided you're a fucking genius."

"No shit," Jagger said. He was busy tasting the purple paint on the inside of my thigh. "Grape."

"You're going to make me jealous," I said. "All of these flavours sound so good."

Jagger looked up at me before motioning to the other two guys. "You heard her, get your pants off."

Mitch and Kage shared a look, but quickly shed their pants and briefs.

After a moment, Jagger did the same, but then he picked up the brush and dipped it into the yellow paint. He gestured for the guys to sit up, and painted several lines and dots first on Mitch's cock, then more tentatively on Kage's.

The head coach sat perfectly still, slightly uncomfortable at first before he started to relax.

"You okay?" I asked him.

He swallowed hard. "Definitely. It's been a while, and never with players who worked under me, but I'm here for it. All of it."

"Of course you are," Jagger said, dabbing purple paint all around the head of Kage's cock, his tongue pressed between his teeth. He did the same to Mitch, then added a touch of pink and a bit of blue.

Finally, he sat back to admire his handiwork and nodded to his satisfaction.

"Your turn," Mitch said. He took the brush from Jagger and quickly smeared several different colours of paint all over his length. And a big dab of yellow on the end of his nose.

"Fucker," Jagger growled playfully. "Now, suck it off."

Mitch grinned and raised himself to his knees to suck the tip of Jagger's nose, deliberately misunderstanding the order.

Jagger snorted. He grabbed the back of Mitch's hand and guided the other centre down to his cock.

Mitch eagerly opened his mouth and lowered it onto Jagger's cock, licking and sucking the paint away. After a moment, and with a small amount of hesitation, he did the same to Kage, taking the head coach's cock deep into his mouth.

Not wanting to be left out, I wriggled around until I could fasten my lips around Mitch's cock, tasting his natural saltiness, mixed with the delicious body paint. The flavour reminded me of a margarita, but much more tasty and addictive.

While I sucked, I watched Kage watching Mitch sucking him off. There was something incredibly erotic about the whole scene. Something slightly illicit about a player giving his head coach a blowjob.

Jagger pulled out a washcloth and washed the rest of the paint off his cock before opening a tube of lube and smearing a large fingerful onto Mitch's rear hole. He gestured for me to move back from Mitch so he could wash his cock clean too.

"Probably not a good idea to have body paint in your pussy." He washed Mitch carefully and then said, "You're going to fuck Eden and I'm going to fuck your ass. Kage is going to keep fucking your mouth."

Mitch nodded and lay over me, his knees between

my thighs. He positioned his cock outside the entrance before sliding himself into me.

Jagger knelt behind him and I felt Mitch move as the other centre pressed his cock into Mitch's ass.

Kage positioned himself beside Mitch and pushed his cock back into his mouth.

Jagger set the pace, thrusting into Mitch, which pushed him deeper into me, and onto Kage.

"If this is your idea of a date, I like it," Kage said. His eyes were half-closed, attention on me and Mitch.

"Me too," I agreed.

Mitch murmured something and grinned around his mouthful. He seemed to also be in agreement. At the same time, he looked to be having the time of his life. He was always outgoing and giving, and what could be more giving than this? Fucking and being fucked. He lived for this as much as he lived to play hockey.

The sound of all three guys grunting and groaning quickly pushed me towards my first orgasm. I arched my back and cried out, muscles clenching around Mitch's cock.

"I'll never get enough of hearing that," Kage said. His voice was strained, with the effort to talk while most of his blood was in his dick. "The sound of Eden coming."

"The sound of me coming is pretty fucking epic," Jagger said. "Mitch too." He fixed his gaze on Kage. "I want to hear how you sound."

"You will," Kage said with a nod. He seemed content

to take his time, sliding in and out between Mitch's lips, savouring the feel of the other guy's mouth.

Jagger gave him a slight frown, but turned his attention back to me and Mitch. He stretched his upper body to speak in Mitch's ear. "Come for me, babe."

Mitch's eyebrows twitched upwards at the endearment, but he moved faster inside me, when Jagger pounded more quickly into him. He let out a moan and a couple of heavy breaths out his nose before sliding his mouth off Kage's cock as he came.

"Fuck… Yeah… Fuck…ahhh." He ground himself into me as hard as he could, eyes crossing with concentration and enjoyment of his orgasm.

Jagger came moments later. Thrusting faster into Mitch's ass before he grunted and fell still, spilling himself into the other centre's rear.

They both flopped forward before Jagger slid himself out of Mitch and let Mitch roll off me.

Their weight was barely off me before Kage was washing his own cock and pulling me over to straddle his hips. He manoeuvred me right above his cock before lowering me down onto him.

"Incredible," he whispered, his eyes screwed shut. "I'll never get enough of being inside you."

"You're welcome," Mitch said with a grin.

Kage cracked an eye open and smiled at him. "You too. I want to feel how tight your ass is some time." He closed his eyes again.

"Any time, Coach," Mitch said. He sat beside us and

resumed licking paint off my nipples and sucking them clean.

Jagger sat on the other side, and slipped a hand between my legs to circle my clit with his fingers while I bounced slowly on Kage's cock.

"I want to hear both of you come," he said. "I like seeing this. Kage's cock deep inside our woman. Right where Mitch just was. I want you to come inside her, add your cum to Mitch's. I want her so full she's ready to overflow." He rubbed harder.

Kage groaned. "I love that. That our woman has had two cocks inside her pussy tonight. She should have all the cocks. Every single one. All she can take."

"She can take all of them," Jagger agreed. "Next time, she will." There didn't seem to be any regret that he'd fucked Mitch the way he had instead of me. We had all the time in the world for them to all come inside my pussy. In the meantime, I'd look forward to it.

All of those thoughts were washed away for a few moments while I came for a second time, quickly followed by a third. The last orgasm, Kage came too, our breaths and bliss in perfect unison.

"Just like that," Jagger said. "Just like I told you to."

Half of the state probably heard me crying out to the sky, letting everyone know exactly how I was feeling and what bliss I was lost in.

Kage was just as loud, grunting and thrusting up into me, spilling his release, letting it mingle with Mitch's.

Finally, we flopped back onto the blanket, puffing and sweating lightly. I lay on top of him for a while until I caught my breath.

"We should get you clean," Mitch said. He gently rolled me off Kage, before parting my thighs with his hands and licking away the cum that leaked out of my pussy.

"That is fucking hot," Jagger whispered.

Mitch's eyes swivelled over toward him, smiling without breaking his rhythm. "Delicious too." He pushed a couple of fingers inside me, worked them around in a circle before sliding them out. He lifted them to Jagger's mouth and pressed them between his lips.

Jagger half closed his eyes and sucked on Mitch's fingers like he'd never tasted anything so good in his life. "That is fucking amazing."

Not wanting him to be left out, Mitch pushed his fingers into me again, before letting Kage taste them. Finally, he dipped them back into me, before pressing them between my lips.

The flavour of my release, combined with theirs was incredible. If we could bottle it, we'd make a fortune. Or better yet, we could keep it amongst ourselves, for our own enjoyment.

He slid his fingers out of my mouth, with a pop, and pushed them back into me, once again working me with his hand and mouth. His expression was a mask of determination. He was going to make me come again no matter what it took, or how hard he had to work my body. Even if he had to work me all night.

I didn't think I could come for a fourth time, but with him touching me like that, and Kage and Jagger exploring my body with their own mouths, licking off paint and sucking my nipples, I shattered again, harder than the other three. Harder than I'd ever come before. I screamed out my pure enjoyment of being the centre of attention of three attractive, muscular men, and the bliss they gave me. I was the luckiest fucking girl on the face of the planet.

Now I had them, there was no way I was letting any of them go.

CHAPTER 18
MITCH

"Hey." I flopped down on the couch beside Jagger.

We still shared the same small house we'd lived in before turning pro. We'd never talked about it, but we were both worried everything we had could go away tomorrow. We could lose our positions on the team roster, or be injured out. Because of that, we never spent much of our money. We could have both bought nice houses by now, but we continued living in this place.

Besides, it was comfortable and familiar. Easier than packing and moving. It was also the perfect analogy for our relationship. Comfortable and familiar, so why change anything? Why move forward? Why not just keep doing what we were doing?

"Hey." Jagger changed the channel when an ad came on. Grimaced and changed it several more times before stopping on one of those shows set in a pawn shop. One guy was trying to convince the owner that his collection of ceramic cows was worth more than the owner was willing to give him.

"Why would anyone pay good money for that shit?" Jagger asked. "You'd stick it in a drawer and forget it existed." He wasn't the sort of person to collect things. Sentimentality wasn't in his nature.

I didn't really collect anything either, because I never used to have the money to do it. I didn't know what I would have collected anyway, apart from books.

"Or on a shelf where it could gather dust," I said. My mother used to have an obsession with dusting. She'd do the whole house at least once every couple of weeks. Whenever she came to visit, she'd do it here. While telling me off for letting so much of it pile up. Personally, I was so used to it, I didn't notice it anymore. What did she expect from house where two men lived?

"Exactly." Jagger changed the channel again.

"Eden liked our date," I said carefully, wanting to open the line of conversation.

"Mmmhmm," he agreed.

"I liked it too," I added.

He nodded, without looking away from the TV. "Me too."

"I figured." He wasn't making this easy. Okay, I didn't expect him to. He was difficult at the best of times, and having personal conversations was never his idea of the best of times.

I cleared my throat. "The four of us fit well together, don't you think?"

"I guess so." He shook his head at the couple on TV who wanted to buy a house for three-point-five million dollars, when she was a teacher and he owned a bakery. He must sell a lot of loaves of bread if they could afford that.

"I think we should do it more often," I said. "Go out with Eden and Kage."

"Sure." He changed the channel three more times.

I pressed my shoulder against his arm and gave him a shove.

"What the hell, man?" He shoved me back and glared at me.

"When are you going to admit how you feel about Eden?" Enough beating around the bush. It was time to get straight to the point. If he'd let me. "And how you feel about me."

"You know how I feel about both of you," he said. He started to turn back to the TV, but I grabbed the remote and switched it off.

"Do I?" I asked. "I know you like fucking us. I know you love it when I suck you off. That's all I know. I'm falling for both of you, but I have no idea how you feel."

"Do I have to paint you a fucking picture?" he growled.

My pulse ratcheted up at the expression on his face. Even when he was angry, especially when he was, he was ridiculously hot. Those dark eyes and smouldering dark looks got me every time.

"A fucking picture would help," I retorted. "Or better yet, a word or two."

He closed his eyes and twisted his mouth to the side. He looked as though he'd prefer to have his pubic hair plucked out one by one, than talk about his feelings.

"If you can't tell me, I guess I have my answer." I pushed up off the couch and started to stalk away.

He grabbed the back of my shirt and hauled me back.

I staggered back a couple of steps before flipping down beside him again. "What?"

"I'm falling for both of you too, okay?" He let go of my shirt, crossed his arms and slumped against the couch cushions. "Are you happy now?"

"I'm halfway there," I said. "Now I need you to tell Eden how you feel. She's coming over after work to have dinner with us; you can tell her then."

He slid me a look, but didn't say anything.

"While we're being so open and honest," I said with a dash of sarcasm. "How do you feel about Kage?"

"Friends," Jagger said. "Only ever friends. Is this where you say you could see yourself falling for him too?"

"Is this where you say you'd be jealous if I did?" I shot back.

He looked at me for a moment through narrowed eyes, then raised his shoulders slightly before dropping them. "No. I saw how you were with him on the beach.

I liked seeing it. If that's what you want, I'm good with it."

"Good, because I'm having a hard time deciding which one of you has a tastier cock." I smiled.

"Definitely me," he said with a grunt. "And you." He seemed to be thinking back to Eden sharing my cum with him. I was hoping he'd try it directly from the source, but I wouldn't push him on that. We made good progress and I didn't want to go backwards now.

"You won't get any argument from me." I grinned. "Eden will be here any minute. I'm going to get dinner started."

He nodded and grabbed the remote to turn the TV back on. A minute and four channels later, he settled on watching a replay of the Opal Springs Dolphins rugby union team.

I shook my head at him indulgently and headed into the kitchen. I took out a tray of chicken breasts and started to slice them, before rolling each slice in flour and setting them aside. In a bowl, I made a quick stir fry sauce, then sliced a bunch of vegetables and put some rice in the steamer. I may not be good at dusting, but my mother made sure I could cook. This chicken stir fry was one of my favourites.

I was just starting to cook the chicken when Eden knocked on the door.

"Come in," I called out. "It's not locked."

She opened the door and stepped inside. "I could have been anyone, coming to abduct you."

I grinned at her over my shoulder. "You can abduct me anytime, babe."

She set her bag down on the table beside the door and came over to give me a quick kiss. "Why do I feel like you'd say that to anyone who wanted to abduct you?"

I laughed. "I try to be accommodating. To be honest, if it was anyone but you or Jagger, they'd bring me back after a couple of hours. I wouldn't be able to stop talking about you two, or hockey. They'd get sick of me like that." I snapped my fingers.

"If anyone gets sick of you, they have bad taste," she said. She tucked several strands of her purple hair behind her ear, and peered into the sauce bowl. "That smells delicious."

"*You* smell delicious," I said. She smelled of lavender and roses. She always smelled good. Good enough to eat.

She turned her face and smiled at me, making my heart melt a little more.

I was wrong when I said I was falling for her. I already had. I was head over cock in love with her. With Jagger too.

"I love you," I blurted out before I could stop myself.

Her eyes widened, but then her expression softened. "I love you too."

I kissed her gently before turning my attention back to the chicken. I didn't want to ruin the moment by burning the dinner.

Once it was perfectly browned, I set it aside to rest while I cooked the vegetables. I tossed them into the pan and started to quickly fry them, turning them frequently with a spatula.

While they cooked, I took a moment to glance over at Jagger. He seemed to be half-watching the game and half-watching us. I raised my eyebrows at him meaningfully, but he grunted and looked away.

I sighed softly and returned the chicken to the pan before adding the sauce to flavour everything. I stirred it through and turned off the stove. I divided the rice between three bowls and added the chicken and vegetable mixture on top.

Eden opened the drawer and pulled out forks for all of us.

Jagger finally turned off the TV and went to the fridge to grab three beers. He handed them around while I handed out bowls and nodded for them to sit down at the table.

I watched carefully as Eden stabbed her fork into a piece of chicken and pushed it into her mouth. She chewed slowly and made a sound of appreciation.

"That's so good," she said after she swallowed. "I had no idea you could cook."

Jagger surprised me by saying, "He's really good. Better than I'd ever be."

"Anyone can cook if they just try," I said. "But I enjoy cooking. It's relaxing." And I liked feeding the people I loved. Seeing them enjoying the meal I prepared was gratifying. Almost as good as scoring a goal.

"I might have to eat here more often," she said. "Brock and I try, but we're not very good at it. Mum used to do all of the cooking."

"You miss her?" I asked gently.

"Yes I do," she admitted. "Sooner or later, I'm going to have to talk to her, which I'm dreading like hell, but I miss her."

"How did she feel about Brock getting you in the divorce?" Jagger asked.

"She didn't mind, but I think that might change when I tell her," Eden said.

"Speaking of telling people things." I kicked Jagger under the table.

He glared at me. "What the hell was that for?"

"You know exactly what it's for," I said. "Go on." I jerked my head towards Eden.

Jagger held his fork in his hand like he might use it on me, but finally he set it down in his bowl and took a sip of beer. "Mitch wants me to tell you how I feel."

"If you don't want to—" Eden started. Her brown eyes were filled with conflicted emotions. She wanted to know how he felt, but she didn't want to force him into anything he wasn't ready for.

I was well aware how long she'd waited for this. How patient she'd been with us both. This conversation was long, long overdue. I wasn't going to let Jagger back out of it now.

"He wants to," I said. I turned one of Jagger's best scowls onto him. I doubted mine was as convincing as his. I didn't have as much practice.

He propped his elbows on the table, laced his fingers together and rested his chin on his knuckles. "I'm in love with both of you." He lowered his hands and went back to eating like he hadn't said a thing.

"I love you too," I said, once I got past the surprise. I hadn't expected that much of an admission from him. Hearing those words from his lips made my heart happy. More than happy, it might burst, it felt so full.

"I love you too," Eden told him. "I'm glad you felt that you could say that to us. It means a lot. Everything." Her eyes were shining, but smiling at the same time.

"Maybe it's time to think about moving," I said. "To a bigger house. Then I could cook for both of you more often."

I thought maybe Jagger would disagree, but he nodded, while never slowing down his eating.

CHAPTER 19
EDEN

We'd talked for a while about the possibility of the guys buying a bigger house, but no one was in a rush to make the move. Even if they started looking straight away, it would take time to find the right place. Time was something we had plenty of. Now we were finally moving forward, I was happy to let things progress at their own pace.

Thinking about moving in with them stuck in my mind for the rest of the night and into the following day. Not just because of the fact I'd be living with them, but that would change things between me and Brock. Things that needed to be worked out before I even considered looking for packing boxes.

All of that was in my mind while I picked up buckets of display flowers from outside of my shop to bring them inside for the night. Sales today had been relatively good, leaving most of the buckets half empty.

I placed two in the corner of the shop and went back for the last two. I reached the door in time to see Brock pick them up and carry them inside for me.

"Thank you." I gestured for him to put them beside the others. "What are you doing here?"

"I just got off work and figured I'd come help you close up." He set the buckets down and leaned against the wall, his arms crossed over his chest.

His intense expression and uniform made my clit throb. Mostly the way his eyes drank me in like I was a fine wine. Or a tasty snack.

"There's not much to do," I said. I turned the sign on the door to 'closed' and stepped over to take the cash out of the register.

"Good. Sit up on the counter." He nodded towards the empty space where I usually wrapped flowers for customers. To the side of that was colourful paper, tape and ribbon. No one walked out of here without a pretty bouquet.

I blinked at him a couple of times. "What?"

"You heard me. Get up on the counter." His tone left no room for argument.

I left the cash where it was and stood on an upturned bucket to hoist myself onto the counter.

He pushed himself off the wall and stalked towards me. His hands on my knees, he slid them up my thighs, pushing my skirt up with them. Parting my legs firmly, he pulled aside the gusset of my panties and lowered his mouth to my pussy. He traced a line from my rear hole to my clit with his tongue.

I placed my hands to either side of me to support me and leaned back, giving him better access to my pussy. He'd told me he'd fuck me with his mouth. I had no doubt that was his only intention in coming here today. To do exactly what he said he'd do. To prove he was a man of his word, if I didn't already know that.

With one hand, he pulled down the front of my shirt and bra and pinched my nipple between his thumb and forefinger.

I glanced towards the front of the shop. People passed every so often, but no one glanced inside. If they did, they'd have a clear view of my former stepfather, his face between my legs. And my bare breast. Maybe I should have been worried about people looking, but I wasn't.

Honestly, part of me hoped someone would stop to watch.

Brock slid his pointer finger inside me, then added his middle finger, caressing my insides while working my clit with deft swipes of his tongue.

I quivered. "I'm going to come."

"Yes, you are," he said between licks. "Come like the slut you are. My slut."

He worked me harder and faster, relentlessly. Neither his fingers nor his tongue were gentle, but I loved it. He'd decided what he was going to do with my body and he was making that happen. Giving me no choice but to come, right there on my workspace. Back arched, crying out his name as pleasure washed over me.

I rolled my hips, grinding my clit against his face, my thighs pressed against the rough stubble of his cheeks. Every movement was beautiful, blissful torture.

With a gasp of breath, I tumbled back down to earth. "That was so…good."

He pressed his fingers into me a few more times, before he slid them out. "Of course it was, pretty slut. That's what your body was made for. Coming on my mouth. Next time, you're going to come on my cock. I'm going to fuck you harder than you've ever been fucked before. And you're going to enjoy it, because your body is mine. Made for me to fuck."

"I want you to fuck me with your cock," I said. "I want to be your slut." In a whisper, I added, "Use me."

"You already are my slut," he said. "You'll get my cock when I'm ready to give it to you. Not before." He rose to his feet and undid the front of his pants. "On your knees."

I adjusted my panties and scrambled off the counter to kneel in front of him.

He grabbed a fistful of my hair and rammed his cock against my lips, forcing me to open my mouth and take him in. Just like he had with my pussy, he was relentless in fucking my mouth. He pushed himself all the way in each time, making me gag. He barely gave me time to breathe.

"Your mouth is fucking perfect," he growled. "So much better than your mother's mouth. She never sucked like you do. She wouldn't let me come down her throat either. But I'm going to come down yours. I'm going to come in your mouth and you're going to swallow every drop."

I looked up at him to acknowledge that I would do what he said. I'd let him do anything he wanted to me. With him, there was absolutely no holding back. I was his to take, to use any way he liked. I wanted to give him everything, like my mother hadn't.

He grunted and pounded into my mouth harder, before letting out a low groan and pressing the head of his cock against the back of my mouth as he came. Hot, salty cum squirted into my mouth, making me gag again before I managed to swallow.

He slid his cock out of me and, his hand still in my hair, hauled me to my feet.

"I've waited so many years for that. It was completely worth it. You're worth it. Your mouth was made for my cock. Next time, it's your pussy's turn."

He kissed me roughly before letting go of my hair. "The only regret I have is not insisting you call me Daddy." He fixed the front of my shirt, pulling that and my bra back into place.

"Brock…" I wasn't sure what I wanted to say.

He raised an eyebrow at me expectantly. "I think the words you're searching for are 'thank you for letting me come, and for fucking my mouth.'"

"Thank you for both of those," I whispered. "I was hoping I'd see you today. Not just because of that." I patted my hair. It must look like a mess right now.

"What about?" He tucked his cock back into his pants and did them up.

I told him about my conversation with Mitch and Jagger the night before. Specifically about the possibility of moving in with them.

"Wherever you go, I go," he said firmly. "It's time I got to know those boys and Kage. Organise something so I can meet them."

"Okay," I said. "I can do that." I was looking forward to it. All four of my guys in one place at the same time. I hoped like hell they'd get along with each other. If they didn't, we were all in for a world of complications. If Brock didn't like the others, he wasn't going to allow me to move in with them. I didn't want to have to fight with him on that. I already knew he wouldn't give in. He had no intention of giving me up now.

I hesitated for a moment before saying, "Kage told me what he and you talked about the other day. He is interested in exploring what might happen between both of you."

"It's not like I'm giving him a choice," Brock said bluntly. "He's going to do what I say, the same way you do. The other two will as well."

"Jagger can be stubborn and dominant himself," I said.

"He's not going to dominate me," Brock said. "I

might allow him to take part, as long as he knows to stay within his boundaries. We'll work that out. Otherwise he's out."

I doubted Jagger would see it that way. Not as easily as Brock seemed to think. I had a feeling the two would butt heads. I hoped, for my sake, they'd work things out quickly. I had no intention of giving any of them up, not now.

"I'm sure everything will be just fine," I said. "I need to get the cash out of the register and lock up for the night."

"I'll keep an eye on the door." He stepped over to it and stood just inside, his arms crossed. No one would try to get past a burly security guard, especially with the hard set expression on his face.

I once asked him why he hadn't become a police officer. He hadn't given me a direct answer, except to say something about preferring to work for himself. I hadn't pushed him on the matter, but he would have been a good cop. No one would have dared to break the law when he was around. I certainly wouldn't. I felt safer just being near him.

I opened the register and pulled out the cash before locking it and heading into my small office to place the cash into the safe. I was just closing and locking it, when I heard voices out in the shop. I was sure I'd put the closed sign on the door, so who could that possibly be? It sounded like a woman.

It sounded like…

I stepped back into the shop to see my mother standing just outside the door. Brock was holding it open and talking to her.

"Oh, there she is." She spotted me and gave me a finger wave. "I thought you might still be here."

"Mum." My heart pounded. "What are you doing here?" Thank fuck she hadn't turned up ten minutes earlier, or she would have found Brock on his knees, his tongue in my pussy. Or me on my knees. Either of those would have been bad. The idea was mortifying.

"I decided to surprise you with a visit to town," she said lightly. "I was just trying to convince Brock to let me in." She patted his cheek before looking back at me. "Are you feeling all right, sweetie? You're looking a little flustered."

I was *feeling* flustered, but I probably looked like I recently had her ex-husband's hand wrapped around my hair. My mouth still tasted of his cum.

I swallowed down the taste and the thought, hoping she didn't see the truth on my face. I was never very good at hiding things from her. She always had a way of seeing through any façade I tried to put up. Of course, she was my mother, she knew me better than anyone. Sometimes that was good, other times it was horrific.

"You can let her in," I said to Brock. Was now the time to broach the subject with her? Could I? I didn't even know where to start.

He gave her the side eye, but opened the door wider.

"Thank you, dear," she said sarcastically. She leaned over to kiss his cheek. She straightened back up and stared at him. "You smell like sex." Her eyes widened. She stared at him, then at me.

Slowly, her face turned pink, then red.

CHAPTER 20
EDEN

"Mum." I put out a hand to her, but she waved me off and stepped back.

She screwed her eyes shut. "Tell me I'm putting two and two together and getting eight. Because there is no way what I think is happening is actually happening. *No way*."

She nodded and opened her eyes. Looked from me to Brock and back again.

"Paula —" Brock started.

She raised her hands in front of her, palms facing him. "I don't want to hear it from you, Brock. Eden, what's going on? Why are you both in here looking messy and stinking of sex?"

"Um." How the hell was I supposed to answer a question like that? There was no point in lying to her, but was she ready to hear the truth? I half hoped Brock would let it out, but he didn't. She needed to hear this from me. She'd never believe it from him anyway. Whatever he said, she'd want me to confirm or deny.

"Brock and I..." I started slowly. "We have a physical relationship. It may become something deeper."

She turned on him. "You're fucking my daughter?" she screeched. "I should have known not to leave you alone with her! Of course you'd take advantage of her. She's missing me and the stability of our family life. I was probably out the door for five minutes when you made a move on her." She curled her hands like they were claws, ready to scratch his eyes out.

"Mum, this is recent," I said quickly, firmly. Hoping like hell she'd listen to me. "We've been getting closer for a while now."

I hadn't realised how close until this conversation. We'd fallen into a pattern like married people, but now we were adding sex into the equation. I always cared about him, but at some point, it had developed into something different. A romantic relationship, not a platonic or even paternal one.

She barely glanced at me. All of her fury was directed at him. "This ends *immediately*. You will not lay another hand on my daughter. Eden can come and live with me and John."

"I'm twenty-seven," I argued. "I get to decide where I live and who I live with. And who I *sleep* with."

She looked sickened. She still didn't glance at me. "You were her stepfather. Can you not see how wrong this is? It's absolutely disgusting. I want you out of my daughter's life."

Up until now, Brock hadn't said anything. He'd stood, stony faced and listened to her ranting. Now, all he said was, "No."

"What do you mean no?" she shrieked. "She's my daughter. You're my ex-husband. How could you possibly think a relationship with her would be okay? What the hell is going through your mind if you believe that?" She shook her head, causing hair to work loose from her dark, messy bun.

"You need help, Brock Edwards." She pointed a finger at him, the tip almost touching his nose. "You need professional help. The kind they give to sexual predators."

He batted her finger away. "I don't need help, Paula. If you see anything wrong with this, you might be the one who needs therapy. Eden and I are consenting adults. We're not related by blood. If we want to fuck each other, we will."

Mum flinched at the word fuck. "You can't be serious." Now she looked at me, disbelief in eyes that were the same colour as mine. "Eden? Tell him. He won't listen to me, but he'll listen to you. Tell him you two cannot be in a relationship together. You were his stepdaughter. He's older than you. He's preying on you. You need to move out of there and get away from him."

She looked absolutely desperate.

"I don't want to get away from him," I said softly. "I

care about him. I like him and I like the way he makes me feel."

"What about those nice hockey boys?" she asked. "Couldn't you choose one of them?"

"I'm seeing them too," I said. "And their head coach." I might as well throw in all the details at this point. The situation couldn't get any worse. She could deal with everything, or not. That was up to her.

She shook her head and stepped back towards the door. "I can't believe what I'm hearing. You sound like a whore."

I resisted the strong urge to slap her, both for the word and her tone of voice. I knew she'd judge me, but this was vicious.

"They don't pay me, Mum," I said coldly. "I fuck them because I want to. Just like you fucked John while you were married to Brock. Did it cross your mind how Brock might feel about you cheating on him? How I might feel about you betraying our...family, as you call it? Who was the whore then?"

Her face paled. "How *dare* you say that to me? I'm your mother." After a moment she added, "This is his influence, isn't it?" She turned back to Brock. "You put these thoughts in her head. You've ruined my sweet daughter."

He actually smiled. "I'm doing my best. She seems to enjoy me ruining her."

Mum looked disgusted to the point she might be physically ill. "You're a repulsive excuse for a man. You never gave a shit about me or our marriage. I don't know why you cared that I cheated on you."

"I didn't care." Brock shrugged one shoulder. "Except that you were a hypocrite. You always accused me of emotionally cheating on you. Because I cared about another woman more than I cared about you. At least I was honest with you about that."

"I shouldn't have married you," she said. "You're the most emotionally unavailable person I've ever met."

"I'm very emotionally available, to the right woman." He turned his face to look right at me.

Mum looked like she'd been slapped across the face. "Eden? You never let yourself fall all the way in love with me because you were already in love…with Eden?" She looked completely disbelieving.

"Why wouldn't I fall in love with Eden?" Brock asked evenly. "She's beautiful, smart, sweet, giving. Everything you're not. And yes, she was always the one I was in love with. I married you so I could be closer to her. Now you're out of the picture, she's in my bed."

Mum's eyes swivelled back and forth between us, like she'd never seen us before. Like standing in front of her were two strangers, not her daughter and her ex-husband.

She took another step towards the door. "How could you do this to me? Both of you. You married me so you could be with my daughter. All the time we were together, you wanted her. Did you sleep together while we were married?"

"Mum, no!" I replied immediately. "I would never have done that to you. Neither would Brock. He made a commitment."

"He made a legal commitment, but his heart was never with me," she said bitterly. The look in her eyes was one I'd never seen before. She looked at me with resentment, as though I was the one who destroyed her marriage.

"I didn't even know he felt that way about me until recently," I said.

Once again, she looked disbelieving. I doubted she'd trust another word that came out of either of our mouths. If I said the sky was blue in the middle of the day, she'd assume it wasn't.

"Eden is right," Brock said. "I didn't tell her anything until a couple of weeks ago. When I got tired of keeping my distance and giving her time to realise what was right under her nose. When I decided to claim what was mine."

Mum shook her head. "You must have known how he felt about you," she hissed at me. "What did you do to make him feel that way about you? He was my husband. You had no right to make him look at you. You *are* a whore."

There was that urge to slap her again, but in the mood she was in, she'd probably have me arrested for assault.

I took a deep breath. "I did absolutely nothing. I was living with you because that was what you wanted me to do. You were the one who moved him in with us before we moved into the place we live in now. You were the one who brought him into our lives. I was busy chasing boys like Mitch and Jagger. Remember my nice hockey boys? Guys like that. Not men like Brock, or even Kage."

She met Kage once or twice before. I remembered now that she flirted with him. Right in front of her present fiancé. John hadn't looked impressed. Kage either, but that didn't deter her. Once a cheater, always a cheater. I felt sorry for John if he actually did marry her, only to have her do to him what she did to Brock. Regardless of Brock's feelings towards me, he had made a commitment to their marriage and he would have held to that if she had. Even if it made him unhappy.

"You must have done something," she insisted. "Married men don't just pine after girls for no reason."

"You pined after John," Brock pointed out. "So much so you apparently couldn't resist taking your clothes off and accidentally falling onto his cock. Something neither Eden or I would have done while I was married to you. Eden did nothing. Nothing except being herself. Something you wouldn't know anything about, because I don't think you've been your true, authentic self a day in your life."

He tilted his head to one side, then the other. "You've had so much work done, I don't know what you actually look like." He straightened his head. "I know this though. It doesn't matter what you look like on the outside. On the inside, you're a massive bitch."

She raised her hand to slap him, but he grabbed her wrist and held it tight enough to make her wince.

"If you lay a hand on me, it's the last fucking thing you do," he growled. "Same goes for you touching Eden. If she still wants to see you after this, that's up to her. But you will be respectful or you can stay the hell away from my woman."

Mum jerked her wrist back away from him. "She is not your woman. She's my daughter. You don't get to tell me how to behave towards her. You're nothing more than a predator. I should go to the police and report you."

Brock barked a laugh. "What for? Eden was an adult when we first met. She's an adult now. If going out with someone younger than you is a crime, then they better arrest half the men on the planet. Including John. Although, arresting him might be a favour to him. He'd be away from you. Right now, the only crime he's committed is having bad taste in women." Brock looked at her like he was repulsed by everything about her.

I couldn't blame him, right now I was feeling sick to my stomach at the things she was saying. If she wasn't careful, I was going to vomit on her shoes. I might not even feel bad about it.

"Marrying you was the biggest mistake I've ever made," Mum said coldly.

"I thought the biggest mistake was having me," I

said. She was starting to make me feel like it. I'd done absolutely nothing wrong and she'd blamed me for everything anyway. She was the one who married a man who didn't love her enough. She was the one who turned her back on that marriage and cheated. She was the one who left. She was the one who made me feel like everyone else in my life might leave, to the point where I was scared to get close to anyone.

She turned icy eyes to me. "That was my second biggest mistake."

She turned on her high heels, pushed out of the door and left the shop, the bells tinkling merrily in her wake.

CHAPTER 21
EDEN

"She said *what?*" Jagger growled. His hand was curled into a fist so tight his knuckles were white. He looked as though he was about to put it straight through the wall. If my mother was here, he might well have punched her in the face.

I wiped my eyes again. "She said I was a whore, and a mistake. I know she was angry, but that…" I shook my head. I couldn't put into words how much it hurt. I felt as though she'd taken a knife and sliced off my skin before covering my flesh in salt. I'd never felt so raw and devastated.

"You're neither of those things." Mitch sat beside me on the couch, his brow heavily creased in an angry frown. He also looked inclined to track down my mother and tear her a new one. "You're amazing, smart and sweet."

"Exactly." Kage sat on the coffee table, in front of me,

his hands resting on his thighs. His eyes were intent on me, more worried than angry. "She had no right to say those things."

"Paula is a bitch." Brock leaned against the wall, his legs crossed at his ankles. "She never could handle the fact I didn't love her enough. This isn't even about Eden. If I was head over heels for her, it would have been inadequate for Paula. She can't handle anything less than two hundred percent of the attention from anyone in the room."

Kage glanced over at him. "That was the impression I got from her. She…" He hesitated. "She asked me to meet with her after the game. When you were working. I declined, of course. Even if she wasn't married at the time, she wasn't my type." His gaze returned to me. "I prefer my women independent, not pushy as fuck."

"She sounds like a needy pain in the ass," Jagger said. He stalked from one side of the room to the other.

"She's always been…high strung," I said. "High maintenance. I guess it's not surprising my father left." I loved my mother, but after the way she spoke to me today, I felt as though she'd torn the rose coloured glasses off my face and thrown them under the first passing car. She probably felt the same way about me. After all, who would think of fucking their mother's ex?

"He should have taken you with him," Jagger said.

"No he shouldn't," Brock said. "It worked out better this way."

"For you." Jagger glared at Brock, unflinching.

Brock returns the glare. "Yes, for me. For Eden too, in the long run. Her father was as high maintenance as her mother. The difference is, she wouldn't have had someone like me in her life to make things more stable."

Jagger snorted. "Eden would have been just fine."

"Can you two stop growling at each other?" I said wearily. "It's been a long enough day without you fighting."

Both of them smirked at each other, like the other was to blame, but they fell quiet, for now.

"This will be a lot easier if we all get along," Mitch agreed. He took my hands and turned me to face him. "I'm sorry she was mean to you. You don't deserve that. I hope you won't let the things she said get to you too much. She was hurt and angry, and lashed out. I'm sure she didn't mean all of that."

"She seemed to mean it." I sniffed. "I don't think she'll ever talk to me again."

"Is that much of a loss?" Kage asked. "I know she's your mother and all, but no one should be treated that way."

"What Coach said," Mitch agreed. "We all get angry sometimes, but we don't usually say things like that. Well, I don't. Jagger does." He cast a sly glance towards the other player.

Jagger stopped pacing to flip him off. "I don't say what I don't mean. If I call you an asshole, it's because you're an asshole. But the stuff Eden's mother said is bullshit."

"Maybe it is, and maybe it's not," I said. I wiped my eyes with a fresh tissue. "Is it normal to have four men in your life that you sleep with?"

"Absolutely it is," Mitch agreed cheerfully. "I see no problem with you having four boyfriends. It's no more strange than me having a girlfriend and a boyfriend." He jerked his head towards Jagger. "Maybe two boyfriends." He glanced toward Kage. "None of that makes me a whore, but I will admit to being a slut. I'm not going to apologise because my mouth loves licking and sucking." He grinned.

His smile was adorable, and would have been contagious under other circumstances. Right now, I felt so crappy, I didn't think I could smile ever again. My heart was in pieces on the floor, indentations from my mother's heels in the exact centre.

"There's nothing wrong with being a slut," I said.

I wished I could remember Brock calling me that in my shop without thinking about what happened straight after. If he hadn't fucked me with his mouth, we might have had a better opportunity to explain things to my mother. Something gentler. Something she might have understood without anger.

Who was I kidding? She would have responded in the same way. She was furious and she'd let loose with a barrage of words and accusations. Nothing we could have done would have changed her reaction. Not unless we hadn't told her anything.

Realistically, sooner or later, she would have found

out anyway. I couldn't have kept it a secret for a few years, just to spare myself from her fury. Maybe, if we waited until John was there, he could have helped calm her down. Or, maybe, he would have seen the real her and run for the hills.

Was that the real Mum though? There was a difference between being highly strung and being nasty. Right? Had she thought those things about me all this time and just hadn't said them?

No, I didn't want to believe that. When she calmed down, I'd try to talk to her again. We might be able to reach some sort of understanding.

"Nothing at all," Kage agreed. "I suspect we all fit into that category. Maybe we need a support group. Sluts Anonymous."

"I think we already are a support group," Mitch said. "But I don't need help to recover from my sluttiness. I prefer to embrace it."

"Me too," Kage agreed after a moment. "You're right, we are a support group. Right now, we're all here to support Eden."

"I appreciate you," I said.

I glanced around at them all, one by one. "How did you know to come here?" Brock and I had returned home and I'd sat down on the couch to cry. The next thing I knew, the guys turned up. Kage even brought bags of food, which was sitting uneaten on the kitchen island.

"We have a group chat," Mitch said. "It was my idea.

Brock messaged the chat and told us what Paula said. We didn't need to be told to come. We wouldn't have been anywhere else."

I glanced over to Brock. "You told them what happened?" I was surprised he'd done that. He must have sent the messages off quickly before following me home in his car.

"You want to be with all of us," Brock said simply. "That includes them being here when you need them." There was something more in his expression.

"It was a test," I guessed. "You wanted to see what they'd do."

He nodded unapologetically. "If they didn't want to be here, I would have deleted them from the group chat." That had a clear double meaning. If they hadn't come to be with me, he would have forced me to end my relationship with them.

"There was no way any of us would have failed that test," Jagger said darkly.

"Be sure you don't in the future," Brock replied. "Eden's happiness is important to me. Anyone who fucks with that, fucks with me."

"Her happiness is important to us too," Kage assured all of us in general. "Whenever she needs us, we'll be there for her. One way or another."

"All the more reason to buy a bigger house where we can all live," Mitch said.

"I don't think we've established that we won't kill each other." Jagger's gaze was intense on Brock.

"I won't kill you if you don't be a dickhead," Brock said. "Eden wants you. For that reason alone, we will get along." He wasn't allowing any room for argument.

"I won't be a dickhead if you don't expect me to do what you tell me," Jagger said. "I don't obey anyone but myself."

Kage arched an eyebrow at him.

"Unless it's related to hockey," Jagger added reluctantly. "Then I listen to my coach. On the ice and off, but not at home."

"I can agree to that," Kage said. "As long as you're prepared to avoid doing anything that would put a strain on our professional relationship. If the team starts to suffer, then we'll have a problem."

"We won't have a problem," Mitch assured him. He gave Jagger a meaningful look. "Right, Jag?"

Jagger grunted. "I won't if you don't."

Mitch grinned. "See, piece of cake. We're going to get along like a house on fire. Not literally. Houses on fire aren't a good thing."

"They really aren't," I agreed. I already felt as though my mother set mine alight.

"You're an idiot," Jagger said to Mitch.

Mitch turned his grin on him. "That's why you love me. Because I'm so fucking adorable. And I put out."

"Yeah, that's why." Jagger rolled his eyes, but he almost smiled back at his boyfriend.

I shook my head at them. If we all moved in together, it would be an interesting challenge. We'd have to have a house big enough for all of us to have our own space to retreat to when the others got to be too much. Jagger might need a room on the opposite side of the house from Brock. At least until they managed to find some common ground. They must have something they both liked, apart from me. One way or another, I'd figure out what it was and make sure they both knew.

"Do you want to talk to your mother again?" Kage asked gently.

I drew in a long, slow breath, then let it out through pursed lips. "Yes, but not for a few days. We both need time to calm down and clear our heads. Otherwise, we're just going to end up yelling at each other, and hurting each other again."

"You're not seeing her tomorrow," Brock said firmly. "I have plans for you."

Jagger turned a narrowed eyed gaze in his direction. "Are you giving Eden a choice to do whatever you think she should do?" He looked as though he was ready to stand between Brock and me, to stop the older man from dragging me away to fuck knows where to do fuck knows what.

I appreciated his concern and had to admit his possessiveness was hot, but Brock wouldn't make me do something I hated. He knew me well enough to have a reasonably good idea of my likes and dislikes. Probably better than I did right now, with my mind in turmoil.

"No," Brock replied, his expression and tone even. "I know what she needs. This will go a long way to making her feel better about her mother being a bitch."

Jagger glanced at me, but I shrugged.

"I'm down for anything that might make me feel better."

How bad could it be after all?

CHAPTER 22
EDEN

Marley groaned. "I have to admit that when Brock contacted me, I was a little dubious. But this… This is bliss." She leaned back in her pedicure chair and closed her eyes while the technician worked on her feet.

"This was exactly what I needed." Cat sat on the other side of me. "Honestly, I'm embarrassed I didn't think of it."

"Me too," Marley agreed.

"Me three," I said. "I have to admit I'm surprised Brock did. I always assumed he thought it was a waste of time and money, when Mum and I used to come here together."

I tried not to choke up at the thought of her, and our spa days. I wasn't going to let that ruin the thoughtful gesture from my boyfriend.

"People can change," Cat said. She should know.

"Maybe he thought it was a waste of money when

your mother did it, but not for you," Marley said. "No offence, but it seems like your mother is spoilt already. Where you, my friend, are not nearly spoilt enough."

"That's sweet of you," I said. "That does sound like the way he thinks."

"He *should* think about putting you first," Cat said.

"Because he caused the trouble in the first place?" I asked. What would have happened if he'd been honest about his feelings for me from the start? I honestly had no idea. I liked him, and I was attracted to him, but back then, our lives were on different courses. At least, I thought they were. Looking back, it seemed like we were always intended to end up here, one way or another.

"I was going to say because you deserve to be pampered," Cat said. "But that does raise a lot of questions. He was really only with her because he wanted to be near you? I can't decide if that's romantic or creepy as fuck."

"What are you talking about?" Marley asked her. "Of course it's romantic as fuck. He held a candle for her for all those years. He did everything he could to be near her and take care of her. I can't think of anything sweeter."

"You find stalkers in romance books sweet," Cat pointed out.

Marley sniffed. "No I don't, I find them hot. What could be hotter than a man who's obsessed with you? One who'll do absolutely everything to be with you, even against all the odds?" She spoke in a dreamy tone.

"If you're talking about my father, I'm going to gag." Cat grimaced. "I've accepted that you're basically my stepmother, but I don't need to hear all the details."

"Maybe I was talking about Shaw," Marley said. "I remember the way he used to watch you whenever you entered a room. His behaviour was bordering on stalkerish."

"It was not," Cat protested. "He was just looking out for me. Just as well he was, or I wouldn't be here now."

"Which brings us back to stalkers being hot as hell," Marley said triumphantly. "And men willing to wait years for a woman are just as hot." She looked over at me and nodded firmly.

"So are men willing to book out an entire beauty salon so we can have a spa day," I said.

According to the owner of the salon, we had nails, facials and massages to come. The works. And then a car would pick us up and take us somewhere else. If I didn't fall asleep from all the spoiling.

"A-fucking-men," Marley agreed. "A man who thinks to involve the woman's two best friends is a good guy in my books. Although, you should have seen the looks I got from Toby and Cole when the car picked me up. I think both of them were also wishing they'd thought of this."

Cat laughed. "Mine are busy spoiling Sophie and hoping we have a good time together. All three of them said I work too much and deserve a break. Especially Shaw."

"That sounds like him," I said. He was one of the most protective men I'd ever met. If anyone so much as laid a finger on her, or looked at her the wrong way, they would have had to deal with him. I wouldn't like to get on the man's wrong side. Brock might threaten to stop people from seeing me, but Shaw would follow through with it.

"We should do this once a month," Marley said. "Just the three of us doing girly things and being looked after."

"It wouldn't surprise me if our guys were cooking up something to beat this," Cat said. "You know how competitive they can be."

"If they want to make competitive spoiling a sport, I'm a willing participant," Marley said with a dreamy smile. "I don't mind at all if they want to work to outdo each other. Bring it on."

"As long as we don't end up spoilt rotten," I said. I didn't want to end up like my mother.

"We couldn't be rotten if we tried," Marley said. "We're way too awesome for that." She put her nose in the air and smiled.

"Yes, we are," I agreed. "But we should spoil the guys in return."

They both looked at me with mock looks of outrage for the suggestion.

"Us? Spoil them?" Marley shook her head playfully. "What will they think of next?"

"Ha ha," I replied. "They deserve it as much as we do. In fact, they'd probably love having a spa day. I can imagine the guys all getting a pedicure. Maybe a facial too."

"They get massages at work," Cat pointed out. "Well, mine do." She pointed a finger at Marley. "I don't want to know if my father gets massages at his work."

Marley grinned. "Okay, then I won't tell you about the shoulder rubs."

Cat grimaced and placed her hands over her ears. In spite of that, her blue eyes shone with amusement.

"Seriously though, there's a difference between a massage for work and a massage for fun," Marley said. "We should definitely bring them next time. This place is big enough for…" She wrinkled her nose in thought. "Thirteen." She pushed her glasses back into place.

Cat lowered her hands. "Is it big enough for all of those egos? That's the real question here."

"I think we could squeeze them all in," I said. I was tempted to call them and try, but my dark mood still lingered and I didn't want to infect anyone with it. With the season starting, the guys had bigger things to worry about than my feelings towards my mother. They wanted to win and bring home the cup. To do that, they needed to stay focused. And they would. Kage would make sure of it.

"There's plenty of room for all of you and your men,

and their egos," the technician who sat at my feet said. Her name tag read 'Nancy.' "If not, we'll fit them in. More men should get pedicures. Especially with bright pink shellac."

The technician beside her, Bella, giggled. "All the bright pink. And bright yellow. Then they'd be fancy."

"I can totally see Cruz with bright yellow toenails," Cat said. "And Easton with bright pink. They're both secure enough in their manhood to wear nail polish."

"I can see Mitch and Kage wearing it, but not Brock," I said. "I don't know about Jagger. It probably depends on which way the wind is blowing. Or if he lets Mitch talk him into it."

I had no objection to men wearing whatever kind of make-up they wanted. Why shouldn't they? We spent enough time putting it on ourselves, they should get to enjoy it too. Although, my guys all seemed to enjoy *ruining* mine.

"Toby would wear it," Marley said. "And Cole. Oliver too, I guess."

"My father would definitely wear nail polish," Cat said. "Especially if it was for charity, or something like that. He let people do a lot of things to him for a good cause."

"Like what?" I asked.

"He's been dunked at the school fair," Cat said. "Every year from when we started, right up until now. He's worn a dress and let people throw tomatoes at him. He plays paintball with the kids with special needs and always lets them win. He gets covered from head to toe with paint. I've started to think there's nothing he wouldn't do for a laugh and to make some money."

"That sounds like Oliver," Marley said. "He's very giving." If she was an emoji, she'd be the ones with heart eyes right now. She was clearly head over heels for him and her other guys.

I used to envy her and Cat, but now I understood all of the complexities of having a relationship like theirs. It was easier to appreciate all the things they'd told me, now I was walking in their shoes. They'd always said the hardest and most important thing was communication, and that wasn't wrong. That was something we'd have to spend the rest of our lives working on.

I surprised myself with that thought. Not about communication, but about the rest of our lives. I hadn't thought much past the next handful of weeks. The guys were already talking about a new house and I wasn't sure if I even caught up to that yet. Now I thought about it, it made perfect sense. Living with all of them and spending as much time with them as I could. Growing my relationship with each of them, while watching theirs develop and deepen.

All of that seemed so simple, now I gave it some serious thought. But there was still one huge obstacle in my way. I wouldn't feel right moving on, moving forward, until I sorted things out with my mother. Even if that meant agreeing never to see each other again.

That would hurt like hell, but at the end of the day it

was her decision. If she didn't want to include me in her life, that was up to her. I had to tell myself it would be her who was missing out if she chose to close that door. I'd have to respect that and move on.

A little voice in the back of my head wanted to cry. I really didn't want to move on without my mother.

I just hoped like hell she'd listen to what I had to say.

CHAPTER 23
BROCK

I looked Eden up and down. She looked absolutely perfect in the outfit I'd left in her bedroom. Her hair and nails were done. She smelled like lavender and *mine*. Exactly as I planned.

"You look beautiful." I grazed my lips over hers and led her out to my car. I wanted to press her up against the side, push up her skirt and fuck her then and there in the street.

But not now. That would happen in time. For now, I wanted to continue to spoil her, the way she deserved to be spoilt.

"You look very handsome yourself." She gave me a glance as I opened the car door to help her inside. She'd always been fiercely independent. It was one of the things I loved about her. She was going to have to understand there were things I'd do for her, like it or not. This was one of them.

I responded with a bland expression, but made a note to punish her for that look. If I wanted to open the door for her, I would. She would have to learn to appreciate that I had manners, even if the other three men in her life didn't. It wasn't that I didn't appreciate and support her independence, but if she thought we'd do things her way, she was mistaken. If she needed a reminder, she'd get one. And another, and another, until she learned.

I closed the door behind her and walked around to the driver's side.

As I started the engine, she asked, "Where are we going?"

"You don't expect me to answer that, do you?" I glanced over at her, my eyes narrowed.

She raised her hands. "I was just asking. I figured you wouldn't tell me, but I couldn't resist."

"Try harder," I told her. I said nothing more as I drove away from the house and through the quickly darkening streets of Opal Springs.

She didn't say anything either, until I pulled up in front of the local bookshop. The place was closed, only a single light burning in the centre of the building.

"No offence, but…" She peered out the window of the car, at the front of the shop.

"None taken." I walked around to her side of the car and opened the door for her before pulling a bundle of keys out of my pocket.

"Are we breaking in?" she asked.

"Would you have a problem with that?" I pressed the code into the security system beside the door, and selected the key to slide into the lock.

"If we get arrested I will," she said. "I don't think the Ghouls' PR department would be very happy if I got caught. I don't think your boss would like it much either."

I looked back at her. "I work for myself."

"Exactly," she said lightly. "You wouldn't like it if you got arrested."

"Then we won't get arrested," I said. I had full permission from the owner to be here tonight, but Eden didn't need to know that. Let her think we were being naughty. She might get off on it. I would have, but she was right, I wouldn't like it if we got arrested for trespassing.

I pushed the door open and ushered her in before closing and locking it behind her.

"Over here." I took her hand and led her to the back of the shop, where a table was already set up. Striking a match from a box on the table, I lit the candle in the centre.

"You're full of surprises," she told me. "I wasn't expecting a romantic dinner in a bookshop."

"You'll need your strength before I fuck you," I told her. I was tempted to skip the food, but I also needed my strength. I'd waited this long, I could wait a little longer.

I pulled out her chair and gestured for her to sit

before pushing it in and taking my own beside her. "I know how much you like spicy food." I lifted the lid on the plate of chicken curry and rice before spooning the food onto our plates.

"This smells incredible," she said. She leaned forward and took a long sniff. "When did you do this? How?"

"I have my ways," I said simply. I handed her a warm piece of naan bread and broke off a section of mine to dip in my curry. The food was blazing hot in my mouth, just the way I liked it. Almost as hot as the woman who sat beside me.

"This is so good," she moaned.

My cock twitched at the sound. If she kept doing that, we wouldn't make it through the meal.

With that in mind, I ate quickly, not caring that it burned all the way down. Every so often, I took sips of wine to cool my mouth. Not enough to get tipsy. I'd be sober when I finally sank my cock into her glorious pussy.

The moment she put down her fork and patted her stomach, I pushed my chair back and took her hand. "You know where the romance section is?" I asked.

"Of course, it's my favourite section," she said. "I love that Amanda, the owner, stocks a huge variety, especially from independent authors. She's very supportive of them."

I knew all of that because I was in charge of the shop's security, and I bought my crime thrillers here.

Amanda always stocked a good selection, and was happy to order in anything on request.

I nodded and walked to the romance section with Eden. It wasn't a section I frequented, to be honest. Not that I looked down upon the genre, but it wasn't my cup of tea. It was hers, so this was where I'd give her something to remember. She'd never come back into this bookshop without thinking about me. About us.

Smiling to myself, I took her other hand and pinned her back against a shelf of romantic paperbacks.

She let out a squeak of surprise. "We're not here to shop, are we?"

I chuckled, deeper now in my chest. "No." One hand curled around her wrists, I tugged down the front of her shirt, and her bra, exposing both of her luscious breasts.

Unable to wait any longer, I leaned down to graze my teeth across one before drawing it into my mouth and sucking.

I pulled up the front of her skirt and pushed her panties aside to rub my fingers across the front of her pussy and down to her clit. "You're so wet already," I said. "Who made you so wet?"

"You did," she whispered. "The whole time we were eating, I was thinking about you touching me."

"Of course you were," I said. "You're my slut. You want me to fuck you, don't you. Don't you?" I demanded when she didn't respond.

"Yes, yes," she said breathlessly. "I want you to fuck me."

I wanted to make her come first, but I couldn't stop myself. I undid the front of my pants and pulled out my cock. My hand curled around one of her thighs, I pressed her back against the books and positioned my cock at the entrance to her pussy. With one smooth stroke, I pushed myself all the way inside my former stepdaughter's tight, wet heat.

I groaned at the feeling of her around me, holding my cock with her muscles. Surrounding me so completely like I'd imagined too many times before.

Only this… This was a million times better than anything I'd ever pictured. Finally, finally after all these years, my cock was inside Eden's body. Where it belonged. Where she belonged, around me.

"You're mine," I told her. "You always have been and you always will be, but now I can claim you fully. The way I should have done a long time ago."

I pushed her back harder still and pounded into her, giving her everything and holding back nothing. Hearing her whimpers and moans as I slammed in over and over, driving us both closer and closer to oblivion.

"Come with me," I insisted. "Show me who you belong to."

She groaned. "Brock…"

My name on her tongue was like heaven. Her pleading tone was bliss.

"Fuck me harder," she begged.

I couldn't resist her any more than I could make myself stop breathing. I gripped her other leg and wrapped both of them around my waist, so I could pound in deeper, harder, relentless.

The whimpers she made before she came made my balls contract before exploding inside her. Shattering us both and filling her glorious body with my cum.

I held her there for the longest time, wanting to enjoy the way she felt.

We'd fuck many, many more times after this, but this first time was something special. Something I wanted to linger in her mind even while she was fucking her other three men. This place would always be special to her because it was the first place I had her.

Every time she walked through the door to buy books, she'd think of me. She'd think of the way she came around my cock when I told her to.

Finally, I lowered her down to the floor and pushed her hair off her face.

"That was everything I knew it would be," I said. "And more."

She smiled softly. "Yes, it was."

I cocked my head at her. "What do you say?"

"Thank you for fucking me," she said.

I straightened my head. "You're welcome. Now, I have one more surprise for you."

"Another one?" she asked.

"For being a good slut, you get another one," I agreed. "We can't leave without a few books, can we?

Choose what you want and I'll organise to pay for them in the morning."

"Orgasms and books," she said. "The perfect date. I hope we didn't mess up the shelf." She turned around to look behind her before straightening the books she'd had her back pressed against.

"It was worth it," I said.

She glanced at me over her shoulder and grinned adorably. "It definitely was."

My cum must have been trickling down the inside of her thighs while she started choosing books. That thought made me start to harden again.

When she'd picked the books she wanted, I'd fuck her mouth.

CHAPTER 24
EDEN

"Thank you for agreeing to meet me for lunch." I sank into the chair opposite my mother. My nerves were as frayed as hell. I thought she'd refuse to see me, or decide not to show up. Now she was here, I was worried she was going to get up and leave.

Yes, I'd lain awake at night thinking about all of these scenarios much more than I probably should have.

"Why wouldn't I?" she asked, as though the answer was obvious. "You're my daughter, Eden. In spite of everything, I do love you."

I bit back the urge to go on the defensive. That wouldn't help. Right now, I needed to be calm and rational. Just like I would have told my best friends to be if they were in my situation.

"I love you too, Mum." I grabbed up the napkin from beside my plate, flicked it out and laid it across my lap.

I picked up the menu and looked at it without seeing anything.

I'd been in here often enough that I knew exactly what I wanted to eat. Not that I had much appetite right now.

"I see you didn't bring Brock or any of the others with you." She looked around me, and around the small restaurant.

"Mitch, Jagger and Kage are at training," I said. "Brock is outside somewhere, hovering."

There was no way he was going to let me come here alone. Not after the other day. He wasn't happy about me being here at all, but he supported my attempt to make amends with her. He, like the other guys, didn't want to see me hurt again.

Neither did I, if I was honest with myself. All of the big feelings I'd been processing since the last conversation with my mother had weighed heavily on my mind. Her words kept replaying around and around. Like a video stuck on replay.

She made an indeterminate noise in the back of her throat and pretended to be interested in her own menu.

Finally, I put mine aside and placed my arms on the table in front of me. I leaned forward and looked her right in the eyes.

"I know finding out about Brock and me was a shock," I started. "It wasn't meant to happen that way."

She put down her own menu and mirrored my pose. "How was it supposed to happen?"

"Not like that," I said. "We would have told you. It was never my intention to keep any secrets from you."

"It seemed to be his intention," she said bitterly. "He kept secrets from the start."

"I know they must have hurt," I said. "If someone told me they were only with me to get closer to someone else, I'd be devastated."

That had to feel like a stab right through the heart.

"He used me," she said bluntly. "He used me to get to my daughter. And now my own daughter is telling me she's all right with that and wants to be with him?"

"It's not all right that he used to you," I said, forcing my voice not to waver. "He should have been honest with you. He should have told you exactly what he felt."

I shook my head. "None of us can undo that now. It sucked, but it's in the past. All I want to do is move forward, and I want that for you too. I want you to be happy with John and not hate me, or Brock, for what happened so long ago."

"I could never hate you." Her eyes shone. "I'm sorry about the things I said. I was caught off guard and I bit back. I shouldn't have done that. It wasn't you I was angry at. It was myself."

I cocked my head at her. "Yourself? I don't understand."

She sighed and picked up her glass of water from beside her plate to take a sip. "I knew he wasn't in love with me. I knew and I didn't walk away. I hoped I could change him. That I could make him fall in love with me. I knew there was no chance of that happening. Eventually I realised that and...I gave up on him. On us." She placed her glass down and stared into it.

"I think I always knew it was you he wanted," she whispered. "I should have confronted him. If I had, it would have saved all of us a lot of heartache and pain." She chewed her lip.

"I used to see the way he looked at you and it drove me crazy. Because all I wanted was for him to look at me that way. But how could I blame him? I have the best, most beautiful daughter in the entire world. How could anyone not fall head over heels in love with you?"

My face heated. "You knew he cared about me?"

She hesitated for a long moment before saying, "I guessed. I used to wonder what you did to make him feel that way about you, but I realised you did absolutely nothing. All you had to do was be sweet, smart and charming, and he'd be eating out of your hand. Nothing I could do would change the fact that I'm not you. As soon as I realised that, I turned away from him. I found a man who wanted me, and looked at me the same way Brock looked at you. And I cheated, because I thought maybe it would upset him. It was my way of getting back at him for not loving me. Every illicit moment felt like... Revenge. In the end, the only person I was hurting was myself. Sometimes I think I don't deserve John."

"He was happy to sleep with a married woman," I

pointed out. I closed my mouth and pressed my lips together. I shouldn't have said that, but it was the truth.

Fortunately, she didn't seem angry at me for pointing that out.

"He was there for me when I needed him," she said. "Don't blame him for my shortcomings."

"I don't," I said quickly. Her shortcomings were her own. I wasn't going to put them on him. He seemed sweet and as far as I could tell, he genuinely loved her. If their start wasn't necessarily perfect…well, neither was mine and Brock's. The messy start didn't matter so much; in the end. It was what we did from here on that mattered.

"Do you think you can bring yourself to support me being with Brock and my other guys?" I asked carefully.

"Can I stop you?" she asked with a laugh.

"As it happens, no," I said. "But I'd rather do life with you on my side, than argue with you."

She leaned over and put her hand on mine. "I want that too. I'm sorry for the things I said. They were inexcusable. I wouldn't have been surprised if you decided never to talk to me again."

"Since Dad left, it's been you and me against the world," I said. "I still want us to be like that. I want you to be in my life."

"I'm glad you do." She glanced down at her plate, then back again. "You might have to give me some time to get used to it, but I support you and Brock being together. Because I know that's what both of you really want. And all I want for you is for all of your dreams to come true."

I placed my hand over hers. "That's what I want for you too."

She smiled. "So tell me about this having four boyfriends stuff. How does it work?"

"Are you looking to add to your relationship?" I asked. "Does John know?"

She gave me a sideways look and a half shrug. "I like to keep him on his toes. Besides, I came to town to tell you something."

"You're not pregnant, are you?" I asked. I'd support her if she was, but the idea of a baby sibling would also take time to get used to.

She snorted. "Of course not. But John and I have a girlfriend and she's pregnant. I wouldn't be opposed to exploring other possibilities. After all, life is too short not to get everything you want."

"That's for sure," I said.

Her news was going to take me a day or so to wrap my head around. I had no idea my mother had a third person in her relationship, but I was happy for them. The baby would be a stepsibling of sorts. They'd certainly grow up with lots, and lots of family and lots of love.

I was happy for them. A person couldn't get too much love.

CHAPTER 25
JAGGER

I leaned against the door frame and watched the other three guys surrounding Eden on the couch in Brock's place.

Mitch sat beside her, looking happier than I'd ever seen him, including when the Ghouls turned pro.

Kage sat beside him, his legs crossed, relaxed as fuck.

I wouldn't admit it, but it felt like he'd been a part of us for a long time. He fitted in like he'd always been here. It was already getting difficult to remember time before him. In time, I'd say the same about Brock.

This was it, the five of us and none of us were going anywhere. We were in this for the long haul, no matter what the world threw at us.

"So we're all in agreement," I stated. "As soon as the season is over, we'll find somewhere to live, all four of us."

Brock replied with a curt nod. "That's what we're doing. I'll rent out my place for additional income. You and Mitch can do the same, or sell, whatever you like. Kage too."

I narrowed my eyes at him. I didn't need his fucking permission to do whatever I wanted to my home, but neither Mitch nor Kage seemed to give a shit about his bossiness.

Kage even nodded. "It makes more sense to live under the same roof, rather than having separate households. It's a lot cheaper."

"And we get to hang out every day," Mitch said happily. "Except when we're travelling for work."

"Then Eden has me to keep her company," Brock said. He looked as though he was looking forward to us being away, so he could have her to himself.

Could I blame him? I guessed not. Any chance I got, I'd keep her to myself too. Or to Mitch and me. I wouldn't object to having him to myself from time to time too. He was a pain in my ass once in a while, but I was used to having him around.

Okay, I loved him as much as I loved Eden, but I wasn't going to stop being my usual, grumpy self for any of them. I was who I was and I didn't need to change for anyone. That was one of the things I loved about the people in this room. They didn't want me to change. Not one of them would have asked me to. Not even Brock, and we were destined to clash here and there.

In the end, we respected each other and wanted the same things. Unity, happiness to the people we loved, and orgasms. Lots and lots of orgasms.

"I can't wait to find somewhere and paint all the walls purple," Eden said.

We all looked over to her and she burst out laughing.

"You should see the expression on your faces." She grinned at us. "Did you really think I meant it?"

"I don't mind if you meant it," Mitch said. "Whatever colour you want the walls, I'm good with it."

Of course he would be. If she wanted a particular star in the sky, he'd try to find a way to get it for her. There was nothing he wouldn't do for her, for any of us. He had the biggest heart of anyone I knew.

"We're not painting the walls purple," Brock said. "A tasteful, off-white will be fine."

"What about pink?" Mitch asked him. "You look like a pink guy."

Brock raised his eyebrows at him. "Absolutely not. Pink is perfect for nipples, not walls."

"Nipple pink walls would be interesting," Kage remarked.

Brock glared at him. "We're not doing that either." As he regarded the head coach, his eyes darkened.

Kage clearly picked up on the vibe. Lightly he asked, "What are we doing then?"

My cock throbbed in response to the increase of

testosterone levels in the room. And anticipation of Brock's answer.

Brock took a moment, drawing out the anticipation before he responded with, "Come over here and get on your knees."

I don't know whose eyebrows shot up faster, mine or Mitch's. Either way, I found myself holding my breath, waiting to see what Kage would do. I thought he might refuse, but then he was on his feet and stepping over to kneel in front of Brock.

We all watched as he undid the front of Brock's jeans, eased the sides apart and freed his erection. With only a glance at Brock's face, Kage lowered his mouth around Brock's cock.

"Well, that's fucking hot," Mitch whispered.

"It really is," Eden said, her voice even lower. Her eyes were wide and dark as she watched Kage's head bob up and down as he sucked.

Brock glanced over at her, then at Mitch. He didn't have to say a word. She crawled over to straddle Mitch's lap, before they started to tear at each other's clothes.

Eden pushed Mitch back and sat with her knees on either side of his hips. He palmed her breasts as she lowered herself onto his cock.

As much fun as watching was, I hurried to grab a tube of lube. I opened the lid and smeared a generous amount onto Eden's rear hole. "I'm going to fuck you here," I told her. "Lean forward."

She glanced at me over her shoulder before doing what I told her to do. Exposing that perfect, puckered hole to me.

I shed my pants and knelt over Mitch's legs. I slipped a finger inside her ass, then another, stretching her and preparing her for me. A third finger went in, followed by a fourth, until her muscles were nice and relaxed.

She really was the perfect slut.

I positioned my cock and slowly and carefully slid inside her. Every couple of seconds, I stopped to let her adjust and get used to having me in there. Bit by bit, I pushed in deeper until she took me all the way to my balls.

"You're so fucking tight," I breathed. I knelt still, waiting for her to fully relax before I started to thrust. I drove into her, setting the rhythm for her to bounce on Mitch.

I glanced over to where Kage was still vigorously sucking Brock, who sat with his eyes half closed enjoying the treatment. If I watched for too long, I was going to come very quickly. Watching my head coach blowing Eden's former stepfather was fucking hot.

My gaze went to Mitch, who was watching with just as much dark eyed interest.

I made a mental note to order a really large bed. We might not want to sleep together every night, but we'd do this again. Giving each other pleasure and taking it in return.

With some amusement, I realised Eden wasn't the only slut here. That description applied to all of us. Living together, we'd be hard a lot of the time. Fucking hardened hearts. And hardened cocks.

"I'm going to come," Mitch said with a groan.

"Me too," Eden said breathlessly.

"Both of you wait," Brock barked. "Do not come until I tell you to."

Mitch moaned. "But—"

"Do as he says," I said. "Wait." He didn't tell me to wait, but I didn't want to rush anyway. Eden's ass felt too good to hurry. I wanted to stay inside her all day long.

Brock looked over at me and gave me a respectful nod, which I returned. Between us, we'd have the other three doing what we told them to do. At least, in the bedroom. I'd work on getting them to obey outside the bedroom and I knew he would too. But we wouldn't tell each other what to do. That was understood and accepted. For now. There was plenty of time for me to work on him.

Brock's breathing came faster and faster. He must have been very close to coming. The closer he got, the more avidly I watched. I very much want to see him come inside my head coach's mouth.

Finally, he said, "Come with me." He came a moment later, thrusting hard into Kage's mouth until the head coach was gagging, but still taking him all the way in.

Mitch and Eden both followed a few moments later. Crying out and gasping and whimpering in pleasure.

I gritted my teeth, forcing myself to hold on for a little longer. Partly because I wanted to, and partly because I didn't want Brock to think I was doing what he told me to do. I was stubborn enough to hang on until Mitch and Eden came down, before I spilled myself into her ass, grinding my hips against her luscious cheeks.

I flopped down against her, enjoying the feeling of being close to her while I caught my breath. Finally, reluctantly, I pulled out of her and helped her to roll off Mitch.

Kage eased his mouth off Brock and swallowed down his release. As he did, I remembered he was yet to come. I raised my eyebrows at Brock, who nodded again.

"Kage, I want to see you fuck Eden."

Kage didn't need to be told twice. Neither did she. She let him lean her over the side of the couch before he pushed down his track pants and rammed his cock inside her.

All three of us watched while he thrust into her, a smile on the corners of his lips. "I've always liked an audience."

"I've always liked watching," Mitch said. "As much as taking part. In fact, I like all of it."

I sat down beside him and put my arms around him

to draw him to me. "I've noticed that about you. Whatever happens, you're ready for it."

"As long as I have you guys, I am." He turned and kissed me.

"You'll always have us," I assured him. "Always."

To the sound of Eden been thoroughly fucked, I held him close, inhaling the scent of him, and her arousal. I'd always be addicted and I didn't give a shit. This was the best addiction of all.

I actually smiled as Eden came again, stealing an orgasm from Kage. The expression on both of their faces was a sight that would always be seared into my brain. Concentration, bliss and love. That was all we needed.

That and each other.

EPILOGUE
KAGE

The game was on a knife's edge in the third period. So were my nerves. We hadn't played the Demons since preseason, not until now. We'd held our own, but the game tonight was as close as it had been then. Neither team was giving the other a centimetre of leeway. Not even a fucking hair.

I stood beside the rink, shouting orders and trying to look cool and calm. If anyone bought it, I was a better actor than I thought I was. On the inside, I was tense as fuck.

More so when I chanced a glance at Aidan Draeger. The man was the stone wall I needed to be. His expression was as guarded as a basket with several goaltenders, each more skilled than the last. If he felt a drop of nerves, he gave no sign. None. His words to his players were short and blunt, all business.

Rather than being intimidated by him, I was

inspired. I needed the same demeanour. The same rapid fire response, with glacial facade. I sucked in a breath and forced a mask into place, hoping it'd hold until the end of the game. Until we won. We'd played plenty of games this season already. Won some, lost others. This felt like the real test. The toughest team in the league and we had each other on the run. Everything to lose. Everything to prove.

No fucking pressure.

I gestured for Mitch and Jagger to switch out, along with Easton and a couple of the other guys. Moments later, they switched back.

Thirty seconds on.

Thirty off.

Take a shot at goal.

Fucking close.

Switch out again.

Defend the goal. Defend!

I wiped a thin layer of sweat from my brow and grabbed up a bottle of water to take a gulp.

Mitch took possession of the puck and flicked it into the Demon's goal like it was nothing. So perfectly effortless, like we'd practiced countless times before.

So easily I almost missed it.

The crowd didn't. They went crazy as the period ended, sending us into overtime.

I stood back from the edge of the ice. Took a moment. Took the time to look up at the box where Eden sat with Brock, Eden's mother and her new stepfather, John. He seemed nice. And smitten. No chance he'd lust after Eden too. Thank fuck for that. Our new home was perfect for five. Six would be a tight fit, like Eden's pussy. Like Mitch's ass.

Eden gave me a wave, which I responded to by raising my water bottle in salute. Then one to Brock. He was a complicated man, but the more I got to know him, the more I liked him. Under the gruff exterior, he was passionate. In and out of the bedroom. Not a moment passed when I didn't know where I stood with him. He made absolutely certain we all knew. He spared few words.

I respected that. Respected him.

"Don't stress, we've got this, Coach," Mitch told me as he took a drink from his own water bottle. "The Demons are going down." He grinned, like he always did. If anything bothered him, he didn't show it. His lighthearted view of the world was refreshing. If any of us was in a mood, he'd drag us out of it soon enough, kicking and screaming if necessary. Especially Jagger. The pair was night and day, but they both had their own light. Mitch was the sun and Jagger was the moon.

Brock was a thundercloud that rumbled ominously, but left us all wet, eventually.

Eden was a flower in spring, always bright and beautiful, always willing to share herself with any of us. To make us shine when we felt dull.

What did that make me then? Maybe I was a dusting of Canadian snow that made everything that little bit more special. The icing on the cake, which the rest baked so lovingly.

Apparently I was a poet now.

I nodded to Mitch. "I know they are. Give 'em hell." I patted his shoulder and smiled, before putting my head coach facade back in place.

"Consider it given," Jagger said before he headed back out to the ice.

Mitch stood beside me, almost close enough to touch as the horn sounded around the ice. A call to battle.

A call the team all met, with faces as stony as mine.

Jagger slapped the puck away the moment it was dropped, driving it to Easton.

Time stopped while Easton turned on his skates and took the shot.

The puck slid across the ice, spinning with its own momentum. It passed straight between the legs of the Demon's goalie before he knew it was there.

The crowd erupted in cheers and screaming.

"We fucking won!" Mitch shouted, almost in my ear.

Forget stony. I was grinning bigger than I ever had. We had each other, and we'd beaten the unbeatable. The Dusk Bay Demons.

No one would doubt the Ghouls deserved their place in the league now. Not us, not anyone. We'd earned it, and we'd proven it.

We owned that fucking ice.

Now we'd take the cup.

. . .

Thank you for reading! If you can't get enough steamy sports RH, check out Filthy Ruck, Ruck Boys book 1.

For a bonus scene of what Brock got up to while Eden was alone in the shower, you can get your copy here.

ABOUT THE AUTHOR

Maggie Alabaster writes reverse harem romance.

She lives in NSW, Australia with one spouse, two daughters, one dog, and countless birds.

Sign up for Maggie's newsletter! Sign Up!

Join Maggie's reader group! Join here!

Follow Maggie on Bookbub! Click here to follow me!

Check out Maggie's website- www.maggiealabaster.com

ALSO BY MAGGIE ALABASTER

Ruck Boys

Filthy Ruck

Sparrow and the Mafia Kings

Possessive

Ruined

Corrupted

Pucking Dark Hearts

Pucking Hearts Collide

Pucking Forbidden Hearts

Pucking Hardened Hearts

Dusk Bay Demons

Puck Drop

Breakaway

Power Play

Brutal Academy

Book 1 Heartless

Book 2 Cruel

Book 3 Vengeful

Court of Blood and Binding

Book 1 Song of Scent and Magic

Book 2 Crown of Mist and Heat

Book 3 Sword of Balm and Shadow

Book 4 Whisper of Frost and Flame

Dark Masque

Book 1 Bait

Book 2 Prey

Book 3 Trap

Saving Abbie

Book 1 Pitch

Book 2 Pound

Book 3 Session

Book 4 Muse

Book 5 Rhythm

Book 6 Encore

Novella Venomous

Saving Abbie books 1-4

Saving Abbie books 4-6 + Venomous

Ruthless Claws

Book 1 Ivory

Book 2 Crimson

Book 3 Elodie

Harmony's Magic

Book 1 Summoned by Fire

Book 2 Summoned by Fate

Book 3 Summoned by Desire

Shifter's Vault

Book 1 Discarded

Book 2 Deceived

Book 3 Disgraced

My Alien Mates

Book 1 Star Warriors

Book 2 Star Defenders

Book 3 Star Protectors

Academy of Modern Magic

Book 1 Digital Magic

Book 2 Virtual Magic

Book 3 Logical Magic

Complete Collection

Summer's Harem

Book 1: Shimmer

Book 2: Glimmer

Book 3: Flicker

Complete collection

Short reads

Taken by the Snowmen

Jingle All the Way

Also by Maggie Alabaster and Erin Yoshikawa

Caught by the Tide

Book 1–Pursued by Shadows

Book 2 Pursued by Darkness

Book 3 Pursued by Monsters